Assassin Town

A Gabby Gordon Mystery

by

Edward F. Finch

Winchilsea Press
Freeport, Illinois

To Cathy
You & Me, and Susan B.

IN THE SPANDREL

Gabby's eyes slowly adjust to the darkness. "Black as the inside of my pocket," Grandpa used to say. Except for a few brief seconds when the intruder's flashlight beam pushes a pale yellow pencil-thin line of light under the door, there is no light in the tight confines of the spandrel. That fact does not lessen the intensity of the debate raging inside Gabby's mind: hit a button on her cell phone so it will light and she can see what wet, sticky goo is on her left hand, or keep her night vision by coping with the unknown wetness.

This is not a debate about a moral issue. It is not a debate about a point of law. It is not even a debate about doing something that might attract the attention of the intruder. At its simplest it is a debate about tolerating something on her hand which she cannot see; she does not know what it is.

Cell in her right hand, wet ooze on her left. Which door has the lady and which the tiger? Did Solomon ever face a problem like this? Do Bertram Russell's logic theories cover this one?

Bringing her hand up to her face she tries to smell it. Vague scent, but the dust inside the spandrel clogs her sinus passages.

Then there is Glenn to consider—her partner in hiding. Does he want to lose his night vision? She can't ask for fear of letting the intruder know where they're hiding. Does he smell the stuff? Does he know what it is? Is it on his hands? Pants? Shoes?

Trying to weigh the risks and rewards of two unknowns is a task, at least in the abstract, that could be one of those mental exercises designed to get you to think through problems. But this is real life—a life and death puzzle—not a topic being batted around a table of friends over a bottle of Bordeaux.

Taking a deep breath while telling herself that it is a deliberate move, not done in panic, she pushes a button and her cell lights up the spandrel. As she recoils from the blood she sees on her left hand, her legs move, causing the manacles attached to the wall to rattle. *The intruder heard that!* Gabby thinks. So much for rationalization; turning on the light did attract attention.

While the cell is still lit, she looks at Glenn, his wide eyes focusing on her bloody hand. In the dying light as her cell starts to go dark she glances up at the facing wall and sees the letters "ICRR" stenciled on back of the paneling. Suddenly oblivious to the blood and the menacing footsteps outside the spandrel, Gabby's mind races as she pieces together this latest clue.

Chapter 1

Gabriel Gordon, an attorney with the firm of Weston and Sanderson in Freeport, Illinois, finds a message on her desk one morning in May 2010. Community Care Haven called because one of its residents wants to speak with her. She is asked to come to the nursing home at her earliest convenience. The resident is John Galway, a name which means nothing to her.

Situated among the rolling hills of northwest Illinois, Freeport is a town of 26,000 plus souls which has a rich industrial heritage. The seat of Stephenson County, Freeport is 100 miles west of Chicago and 48 miles south of Madison, Wisconsin.

Calls such as this are not out of the ordinary for Gabby, as she is known to family and friends. Her law practice concentrates on wills, estate planning and those legal matters revolving around people trying to provide for those they will leave behind. Not knowing exactly what she will find, that afternoon Gabby dutifully drives across town to The Haven, as it is commonly called by Freeporters.

"You'll probably have trouble talkin'," says the thirtyish CNA as she leads the way to Galway's room. "He's got dementia, but he's actually coherent for brief periods some days."

"Is this a time when he is generally coherent?"

"His sane periods are random, so it's tough to say. If they coulda predicted his swings they woulda." As they enter Galway's room the CNA says, "Mr. Galway? Mr. Galway, this is Gabriel Gordon, the lawyer you asked to have called."

An elderly man looks up from a wheelchair which faces a window looking out onto the courtyard between the wings of the nursing home. Gabby notices that he is a reduced whisper of what had once been a large, powerful man. He sits hunched over; his ninety years seem to press him down. Thin gray hair covers a head which is approaching baldness. Green eyes seem wary, sizing her up as she enters the room.

7

Extending her hand, Gabby smiles as she walks toward Galway. The man makes no move to acknowledge her. He simply looks at the CNA, nods to the door with his head and turns his gaze back to the window.

After the CNA leaves, closing the door as she goes, Gabby looks for a place to sit. The only other chair in the room is against the wall at a right angle to Galway. Unsure about moving it, she sits in the chair where it is. All she can see of Galway is profile.

"Mr. Galway, you asked to see me. How may I help you?"

Long silence ensues during which the man does not move. Gabby is about to repeat her query when he speaks.

"Find anythin' of interest while fixin' her up?"

"Fixing what up?"

"Babcook."

"You are familiar with Babcook Manor?"

"Lived there forty years."

"Really, I had no idea. Are you related to the Babcook family?"

"Hell, no! Not related to no one no more, 'cept my silly-assed sister down in Florida. Hope she still thinks me dead. How'd a woman end up workin' on a house? Got a husband?"

"No husband. My father is a carpenter and he taught me. So, even though I practice law, I enjoy spending my spare time rehabbing old houses. I guess you could call it a hobby."

"Hrrumph!"

"When did you move out?"

"'Bout eight years ago. My wife caught that Alzheimer shit, so I had to bring her here and I needed to stay close to her. So, 'twas simpler for me to just come along, too."

"You don't seem to be suffering from dementia as the CNA said."

"Oh, I needed an excuse to stay near Mary Alice, so been pretendin'. Though some days anymore I've a hard time tellin' when I'm actin' and when I ain't."

"Is Mrs. Galway still here?"

A long silence again, but eventually he speaks softly, "She passed away two years ago."

"I'm sorry for your loss."

Another lengthy pause. When Gabby decides that he is not going to respond, she continues, "So, do you want an update on how I've fixed up the place?"

"Not unless ya got somethin' to tell me 'bout anythin' ya found of interest in there."

"Except for the old furniture in the basement, there was nothing to find, the rest of the house was empty. I plan to give it all to Goodwill, but if it belongs to you, I can..."

"'Bout all it was good for. All older than the hills and pretty worn down. We didn't spend any money on such the whole time we lived there. Matter of fact, we never left the property, not once the last ten or so years we was there. Didn't even go out in the yard the last couple years."

"How long did you say you lived there?"

"Most of those forty years."

"How long in the basement?"

"Forty years."

With a sense of shock, Gabby blurts, "Why?"

"Seems you'll have to work that out. If you'd found somethin' interestin' in there, ya might be askin' different questions now."

"I must admit that I was puzzled by the fact that all of the first floor windows were nailed shut with sixteen penny nails and that the chain link fence was buried two feet underground besides being eight feet above."

"Not what I'm talkin' 'bout. You're describin' symptoms, not causes."

"I couldn't begin to guess where or what I could have found that would have caused someone to nail closed windows or install a fence two feet below grade. It was expensive removing the concrete settings for the posts and all."

"Wasn't supposed to be easy to take out. That was the point. Have ya noticed anyone watchin' the house? Same car drivin' by slowly several times each day?"

"No, but I'm usually only in the house on weekends and evenings."

"Never spent the night in the house?"

"No. It made more sense to fix-up the apartment over the garage and then live there."

"Find anythin' of interest in the garage?"

"Can't say as I did. Nothing that I recall."

"Ever see or hear anyone sneakin' 'round the grounds at night?"

"Not really. Oh, there have been neighborhood kids once in a while, but they were just curious. There are lots of rumors about the place, so people are naturally going to snoop around some."

"Well, call it what ya want. Nothin' ordinary 'bout the garage?"

"No. I been living there since I bought the property. I never intended to live in the house, just fix it up and then sell it."

At that he abruptly turns his chair and looks her fully in the face.

"Best you sort this out before ya sell, Missy."

"But how am I supposed to 'sort' it out and what exactly needs sorting out?"

Another lengthy pause as he seems to carefully consider what he'll say next.

"That attic above the garage apartment—things may not be what they seem." With that he turns his chair so that his back is toward her and he begins to scream, "Mary Alice! Where the hell are you? Its supper time and I needs have some food. Mary Alice, you no good Irish whore, get your ass in here with my lunch!"

The door swings open as the same CNA comes in—she must have been just outside.

"Mr. Galway, ya know Mary Alice is no longer wid us," the CNA says soothingly as she motions with her head for Gabby to leave.

As Gabby passes the nurses' station at the junction of the two wings, she can still hear Galway screaming obscenities at the top of his lungs.

"Good time to be getting out," mumbles a man mopping the floor. "He's got a mean and vicious temper. Even when he's sane he has an orneriness in him."

Gabby merely nods as she keeps walking.

Chapter 2

Sitting in her car in the parking lot of The Haven, Gabby replays in her mind the conversation with John Galway. The more she reviews it, the more bizarre it becomes. She has to admit that she knows very little about the history of the house and certainly does not know who had lived in it other than the original owner—P. W. Babcook. And she doesn't even know much about him.

Gabby's ex-husband Tom had taken care of the deed and mortgage, which she now recalls had some tangled legal issues. And how did Galway know to call her? Perhaps someone told him she had purchased the house. *Small town— short grape vine.*

It is obvious, however, that she needs more information before she can seriously consider Galway's ominous warning about getting it "sorted out" before she sells the place. She is sure they had been told that no one had lived in the house for at least thirty years. *Perhaps Galway has some legal claim to the property that Tom overlooked when we purchased the place. He certainly had his mind elsewhere at the time.*

As she drives out of the parking lot and onto Galena Avenue headed back to her office, she remembers someone who might have answers. Continuing through downtown she turns south on Carroll Avenue and is soon at the entrance to the Stephenson County Museum. *It's possible*, her thoughts run, *Dr. Barnes might be in even though the museum is closed Mondays.*

In her second year with the firm they sent her to the Highland Leadership Institute where she met Dr. H. Elmer Barnes, the museum director. He presented a program on local history and early leaders in the county. The year-long leadership program motivated Gabby to serve on the board of the museum, a move of which her employers approved as the senior partners wanted all of its attorneys involved in community organizations. Groups such as Rotary or Kiwanis do not appeal to her, so when Dr. Barnes asked her about taking a vacant seat on the museum's board, she agreed. She left the board at the end of her three year term. While maintaining her membership in the Museum, she had not attended a single event since.

As she predicted, the lights in the museum office are on. Barnes meets her at the door, warmly welcoming her.

"Well, Gabriel, how nice to see you. It has been some time since you graced the museum with your presence."

"Good to see you, too. Yes, it has been a few years since I've been here."

"Well, my dear, come in and I'll put on the kettle." Any visit with Barnes involves a cup of tea. Most people prefer to do business with him by phone if possible in order to avoid the time consuming "spot o' tea." In his mind taking the time for talk over a cup of tea is the hallmark of a more civilized and less pressured life.

To say that Barnes is of the "old school" is an understatement. He is always nattily dressed in a bow tie, Oxford cloth shirt, a tailored double breasted navy blue blazer and khaki slacks. When outdoors he wears a fedora that even Spencer Tracy would have envied, and he always carries a walking stick. Having worked for the Smithsonian for over thirty-years Barnes retired to Freeport where he was soon hired by the museum as its director. Few towns the size of Freeport could afford a fulltime museum director, let alone one with a Ph.D. and a pedigree as a rare book curator at the Smithsonian.

"Assuming that you have not come to volunteer to rejoin the Board, what is it you need?" Barnes asks as he hands Gabby a cup of Earl Grey, his favorite.

"Did my departure leave you with the impression that I was unhappy as a board member?"

"How could you not have been: three hour-long internecine meetings discussing the color of napkins for the Christmas Tea? I was ready to leave, too. Fortunately, we have moved well beyond that in the last few years. I think you would find the experience much improved, but again, with what may we be of assistance?"

"Babcook Manor…"

"Aha! I knew sooner or later we'd have a conversation about it when I heard you had made the purchase. Now, let me see, I have a folder of materials I prepared for this eventuality. It is around here somewhere."

As Barnes rummages through piles of file folders and heaps of paper, Gabby marvels at the total disorganization of his office. For a man who takes such pride in his personal appearance, his office is always a total disaster. Much sooner than Gabby would have guessed given the seeming state of chaos on the desk, however, Barnes retrieves the folder and hands it to her.

"You see, my dear, I had been working on a history of Babcook Manor for several years, although in this job there is nothing which can occupy one's attention for very long because of the frequent and numerous interruptions. I planned an article for our newsletter, but I ran into several dead ends and I was never able to complete it."

"There's an early history of the house with some photos and the background on P.W., but not much else," Gabby notes as she leafs through the folder.

"Ah, that is true. There is a single sheet on which I compiled a list of 'rumors' about the place, but I have been generally unable to confirm or disprove most of them. In purchasing the Manor perhaps some of those questions could be answered by the property's title abstract."

"I've not seen one. For the most part no one uses them anymore. To save the costs of updating abstracts we rely on title insurance."

"Mores' the pity for historians wanting to trace the history of a property. Anyway, what I have been able to extract, mostly from the will of P.W., is that he left the property to the Catholic Diocese of Rockford. But there was a provision that his son and daughter be permitted to live there until they decided to move or died. P.W.'s son appears to have suffered from some mental defect. I surmise that the poor lad may have had Downs' Syndrome, which today is not considered something for which children who have it are kept from public view, but in the first half of the twentieth century, the poor lad was probably locked away most of his life.

"P.W. was heartbroken that he did not have a son to whom he could hand his industrial empire. He probably felt the unfortunate child was God's punishment for the sin of divorcing his first wife and then marrying a much younger woman with whom he had been having an affair. His daughter Ethel was from his first marriage; the son was issue of the second Mrs. Babcook. Ethel, who never married, appears to have taken on the task of caring for her half-brother after their father died. Ethel and PW, Jr. lived in the house until they died--he in 1950 and she two years later."

"Did Ethel take care of PW, Jr., all on her own?"

"Heavens, no. A lady of her social and economic standing in the early-1950s would not have thought of such a thing. There was a live-in cook / housekeeper who resided in the basement, and some sort of gardener / handyman who lived above the garage. Now, after Ethel died, the property went to the Diocese and there were plans to build a new St. Vincent Orphanage, as well as a home for mentally challenged adults on the property, which was ironic given how PW, Jr. was treated. In '52, when Ethel died, the property consisted of some forty acres."

"I take it the orphanage idea was scuttled?"

"It would seem so. The trend in caring for orphans was away from institutionalization, which is the reason that the existing St. Vincent's Orphanage eventually became Provena Saint Joseph Center, a facility for the aged. Did you know that I was raised at St. Vincent Orphanage?"

"I had no idea."

"Ancient history, as they say. But with the decision not to build a new orphanage the Diocese was stuck with the Babcook property. According to rumor, it was taken off their hands for a very handsome price by a person from Chicago, one Michael Joseph Flaherty. He was a very devout Catholic and a seemingly successful businessman, who was also one of the leading kingpins in what is often referred to in the newspapers of the day as the Irish Mafia. An oxymoron of ethnic terms, but clearly he headed an organized crime syndicate consisting mostly of his Celtic clansmen."

"That explains why people are always telling me that the Mafia used the place as a hideout."

"Most definitely, my dear. I interviewed a man who did much of the renovation on the place for Flaherty and he confirmed some facts. The property that was sold by the Diocese to Flaherty consisted of the five or so acres there today. The rest of the land was sold to real estate developers who went on to build the subdivisions that now surround your property on three sides. Oh, please forgive my manners. Would you care for another cup of tea?"

"Thank you, I'm driving, so I better not. What kinds of renovation work did this guy do?"

"Phil Connors is his name. He worked on the house, along with his father and brother for the better part of two years. That was around 1955. Their work was all inside and consisted of modernizing the plumbing and wiring, as well as stripping the woodwork as all of the original finish had been painted over."

"That must have been a heck of a lot of work. The house has wood trim everywhere. I guess I should be thankful that I was not stuck doing that, too."

"As I said, it took the three of them over two years. Perhaps more interesting is that he said that Flaherty had a pad poured for a helicopter, which the family used in their travels out here from Chicago. I've always thought that a curious fact. Did you know that in the mid-1950s helicopters were still considered somewhat unreliable? The Secret Service refused to use them as a means to evacuate the president in the event of nuclear attack. But again I digress.

"He also said that they found that the paneling used in the basement apartment, which was where the cook lived, came from the Illinois Central Rail Road. My investigation showed that old man Babcook had once had the IC build him his own rail car, but when he had the manor built, he had beautiful wood from the luxury car used in the house, including the basement. I suppose being wealthy means you can still skimp here and there by reusing materials.

"Anyway, Connors told me, it's all there in my notes of the interview, that there were armed guards patrolling the grounds at all times. Only he and his father and brother were allowed in and out without scrutiny. He said that whenever any other workman, like those who built the swimming pool and tennis court came on the property, the day after they finished all three of the phone lines coming into the property were changed. Most curious, don't you think?"

"So what happened to Flaherty?"

"Oh, dear. He was found floating face down in the Chicago River. Apparently the cement galoshes with which he had been fitted were too big, so he just came out of them and popped up to the surface."

"When was that?"

"1959, I believe. It'll be there in my notes. I acquired a copy of Flaherty's obituary from the Chicago *Tribune* and a couple stories on his death."

"So what happened to the property after Flaherty's demise?"

"That's where the trail runs cold, as the detectives in the novels are wont to say," intones Barnes as he wags his index finger in the air. "As I've mentioned before, if I could have a look at the abstract, then I could determine who owned the property after Flaherty."

"There have to be records somewhere. The taxes would have to be paid. Perhaps the Flaherty family held onto it."

"If they did, then they did little to maintain it over the years."

"That's a certainty. When I acquired the place it was heavily over grown. There was an eight foot high chain linked fence around the immediate area of the house, and that fence had another two feet buried below ground. There were two gates in the fence, both of which had double gates, like something you'd see at a prison. Besides the close-in fence, there was another eight foot chain link fence on the entire perimeter of the property."

"That would have been the one that Flaherty had installed. Phil mentioned it in his interview."

"Most of it was heavily rusted and there were gaps in places. In addition, the over grown nature of the grounds had led to several spots where the outer fence had been breached by falling trees and limbs."

"I did check the city directories for the names of people residing there, but since the property was outside the city limits, it was never listed, even when P.W. was living there."

"Well, Doctor, thank you for your time, for the tea, and for the file. I'll get these photographs back to you."

"No need, my dear. The originals have been scanned and those are prints from the scans. The originals are all in our archives, safe and sound."

As Gabby drives off the museum grounds she begins a mental list of questions:

- *Is Galway somehow related to Flaherty?*
- *If not, then how did he come to live there? Squatter?*
- *Why didn't he just tell me what he thinks I ought to know?*

Maybe he's having more periods of dementia than he realizes and has done nothing but send me on a snipe hunt. All of this is all odd, very odd.

Chapter 3

L ater in the day, after her meetings with Galway and Barnes, Gabby sits at her desk staring at the file Barnes gave her. As she reads the notes, she constantly twirls a pencil around her right thumb, a habit she developed as a high school debater. Those who know her well learn not to interrupt her when she is pencil or pen twirling—that is when she is fully concentrating on the problem at hand.

Barnes' file contains several photos of the exterior of the house, probably taken soon after the house was built—the trees are much bigger now. There is a copy of a 1939 Christmas card which shows P.W. and his second wife, Estelle sitting in front of the fireplace in the library. Then there is a photo of him at his desk with numerous floral arrangements around the room. *P.W. looks sad and worn down*, Gabby muses. The note on the back confirms her observation. It was taken soon after the death of Estelle, but on his 80th birthday. He would be dead within three months. Examination of the pictures is interrupted by a knock on the door.

Sam, Gabby's secretary sticks her head in, "Your one o'clock appointment is here."

"Show him in."

"Good afternoon, I am Gabriel Gordon. You must be Vincent Herrswick?" Gabby shakes hands with a man in his mid-fifties. He is gray at the temples and sports designer eye wear as well as very sharply creased suit pants.

"Yes. Thank you for seeing me on such short notice," Herrswick begins. "I keep a very tight schedule and this time slot worked best for me."

"Please have a seat. Can we get you a cup of coffee, a soft drink?"

"No. This shouldn't take very long. I drove in from Milwaukee to see you and I have a very busy schedule with my business and all. Now, as I told you when I made the appointment, I am one of the two nephews of Henrietta Blake, whose Will you drew up and are now preparing for Probate."

"Yes, Mrs. Blake was a delightful lady and we had many enjoyable conversations. Her passing was very sad."

"Well, she was eighty-eight after all and she did have a tendency to ramble on and on about the 'old days,' as she called them, but I have come to ask if you can explain why she left my brother everything and she left me nothing but a family photo from her eighty-fifth birthday, a party which I did not attend because it did not fit into my very tight schedule, so I was shocked and angered when I received a copy of her Will and the photo in the mail last week since my brother and I are her only living relatives."

Gabby thinks to herself: *does this guy always speak in run-on sentences? At least a pause for a breath now and then would put some punctuation in his speech. Even in high school debates I never heard anyone speak this fast.*

"Time is money, Miss Gordon," Herrswick comments as he breaks in on her reverie.

"Sorry. It would seem, Mr. Herrswick, that Mrs. Blake anticipated your reaction. She left this for you in the event you contacted me." With that Gabby hands Herrswick a small envelope, about the size of a party invitation.

Herrswick tears open the envelope and then reads the hand-written note on the card inside.

Throwing the envelope and its content on Gabby's desk, he stands, adjusts his custom tailored suit coat and then says, "That miserly old bitch because I didn't send her a birthday card she cuts me out of my share of two million dollars well I have a business to run and no time for the bullshit from some doddering old biddy so you will hear from my lawyers as I plan on contesting her Will and to think I took the time to drive here all the way from Milwaukee to be insulted by someone who was nothing but an time waster." With that he storms out of the office.

Gabby reaches down and picks up the note.

Vincent, I know you'll be angry, but if you didn't have room for me in your busy schedule, why should I have room for you in my Will? I pray that someday you'll understand why I did this. With Warmest Regards, Aunt Henrietta.

As she places the note back in the file marked "Blake, Henrietta Marie – 1924-2010" Gabby thoughts run to: *If the jerk plans on contesting the Will, he probably will not want this note to be used as evidence as to Henrietta's state of mind when she revised her Will just a week after that birthday party. This would be a nasty surprise for someone who has so little time.*

If she ever thought about it for very long, Gabby would have been surprised that she ended up specializing in wills, estate planning and related legal work. In high school, college and law school she envisioned herself as a litigator, arguing cases before the Supreme Court, setting the legal world abuzz with the brilliance of her arguments, as well as the acuity of her legal stratagems. During mock trials in law school she earned a reputation as a "go for the jugular" competitor.

She never regrets the work she does, preparing each document as if she were writing a brief for an appellate court. She seldom writes a statement without thinking of the possible responses or counter arguments that could be made against it. Perhaps that is also why she so enjoys carpentry. A well-reasoned argument has a lot in common with the hand-made dove tailing on a cabinet drawer.

Chapter 4

That evening, as Billy Joel's song "Honesty" comes from her CD-player, Gabby drops her hammer and nail-punch into their slots on her tool belt and leans back on her haunches to gaze across the dining room floor of Babcook Manor. Three hours of non-stop work making sure that no nail head pokes above the surface of the oak floor. Gabby is determined not to expend any more money than absolutely necessary to complete this project, so she labors every night and all weekends to make the house marketable.

Then what? For three years she has been working on this restoration. *A labor of love or an obsession?* The jury is still out on that one. "Their" plan had been to buy the 1925 French Normandy style mansion, rehab it and then flip it for a profit. But, as her Dad is fond of saying, "The best laid plans…" While wrestling with the reality of her divorce, the remodeling became the release for her anger and anguish, as well as a way of showing, at least to herself that she could bring it off— on her own!

The last room is now close to completion. She wishes she had the resources to hire someone to do the work, but she's exhausted both her personal finances and her credit line in order to get this close to completion.

Living in the small apartment above the mansion's two-story three-car detached garage since the divorce, she cannot afford an apartment elsewhere, on top of the cost of the rehab and the mortgage payments, all on her salary. Having been abandoned for some forty years the house had been a bargain, but still beyond the profit she and her Ex turned on their first rehab project. Finally, she has reached the point where she can put the house on the market, but there will be little profit. If she is lucky, in today's constricted real estate market it will sell for what is owed on the two mortgages.

Without her Ex's physical help she has been forced to hire out far too much of the work—especially landscaping and fence replacements. A God-send has been her father and mother who gave up many, many weekends to help her with the work. While Gabby's father is a carpenter, he is at the age where working a forty hour week and then spending twenty hours on weekends helping her is demanding things of his body it can no longer provide. Any profit margin that might have been realized would quickly crumble if she calculated the sweat equity, but perhaps she should look at it all as being in lieu of the cost of a therapist.

Tools put away, she trudges up the stairs of the garage with the idea of a very hot shower to sooth the muscles aching from long hours on her knees. The question of selling the property—all 5 acres of fenced-in lawn, swimming pool and tennis court each with those very odd twelve-foot high brick walls around them but sans roofs—is still unsettled in her mind. She can't get over a feeling that selling the house could be a mistake, even before Galway's warning. *But what is a divorcee with no children going to do with a house this big?*

Chapter 5

A very successful high school debater, Gabby aimed for law school from an early age. She was recruited on a debate scholarship to the University of Illinois, but left the team before her first season started. Totally disillusioned with collegiate debate and its emphasis on games theory rather than reasoned argument and communication, Gabby worked many long hours at a bookstore all through college to replace the lost scholarship.

At 5' 11" with shoulder length auburn hair and green eyes that reflect her Gaelic heritage, her pert figure draws attention in most settings—though she detests the word "pert." Aware that her looks can easily allow her to maneuver around the average distracted male in a position of power, she disdains any such use, though she frequently questions the ethics of whether she could do better for her clients if she relied more on her physical assets in negotiations rather than the strength of her legal arguments. But her chief pleasure, next to carpentry work, is navigating thick legal issues.

Two years after arriving in Freeport she met Tom Reining, a freshly minted attorney, also hired by Weston and Sanderson. Six months after his arrival Gabby and Tom discovered their mutual passion—house renovations. Together they purchased a very run-down 1880s Italianate style house on West Stephenson Street and begin a rehab. Working together evenings and weekends led to a romantic relationship that ended in marriage eighteen months after they stripped out the first of the old plaster. Gabby used to joke about not needing a wedding veil given all the plaster dust in her hair.

Gabby and Tom shared a family background in carpentry. His father was a contractor who put Tom to work summers during high school and college. Gabby's father insisted his only child would know how to work with wood even as she dreamed for law school. For Gabby the joy of physical labor employed in carpentry work will remain with her the rest of her life. She never needs to make time for gym workouts as all her spare time is devoted to one building project or another from the time she was admitted to the bar.

When the Stephenson Street house was completed, they sold it for a good profit and began looking for another project. That led them to Babcook Manor, a light tan brick six-bedroom house located on the city's eastern edge. A primary feature of the house is a turret that covers the front porch on the ground floor and provides a unique reading room off the master bedroom. A very large bronze letter "B" is mounted on the turret at a level with the second floor. It is flanked on both sides by narrow vertical windows that look like the openings used by archers in castles.

W. P. Babcook was a wealthy industrialist who built the residence when its location was over a mile outside the city. Now it is surrounded by the city, an island of green isolation amid sprawling subdivisions.

As Gabby eases into her bed, the heat from the shower having washed away both the sweat and the aches of the evening's hard labor, the idea of selling Babcook Manor lingers in her mind. She cannot afford to keep it, but something keeps telling her that she must not sell.

Chapter 6

As she lays awake staring at the ceiling of her bedroom, Gabby keeps replaying the day's conversations. Annoyed with herself for being unable to unwind and attain some much needed sleep, she casts about for a distraction. In that, she realizes that she does not own a TV and that she has not been to a movie or read anything other than work related materials for uncounted years. Her outdated "boom box" is permanently tuned to AM radio so she can listen to the Cubs and Bears, when it doesn't have one of her Billy Joel CDs playing.

Eventually Galway's pronouncement about the attic space above the second floor of the garage comes to her, so she gets up, pulls on her usual work clothes—denim blue jeans and a denim shirt so faded that the blue has turned to a pale grey—and a well-worn, sweat stained Chicago Cubs ball cap with her hair in a ponytail pulled through the adjustment strap in the back. The cap had been a promotional give-away when she went to a Cubs home game with her dad-the summer before she entered law school.

Dressed, she goes down to the first floor of the garage to retrieve a step ladder and a flashlight. The opening to the attic space is in the closet of her bedroom. With flashlight in hand, she pushes open the piece of plywood used as a covering, only to get a face full of insulation as the suction of the moving plywood pulls pink wisps of spun fiberglass back into the closet. *Shit and shoved in it...should have worn eye protection.*

She recalls insulating this attic after she replaced some of the wiring three years before. She left the old shredded-style insulation in place and simply unrolled the new fiberglass product over the top.

With her head well into the opening, her eyes follow the areas illuminated by her flashlight, as she slowly scans the entire space. Nothing seems out of the ordinary. Nor can she recall thinking anything was odd when she scrambled around up here before.

But Galway said something about things not being what they seemed. A second perusal of the attic causes her to sense that the gable end over her bedroom appears to be closer than it did when she was standing in the closet looking in the same direction into the bedroom. Crawling across the joists, she scrambles to that gable end. The wood sheathing seems newer. Looking back at the other gable end, she can see that the sheathing there is darker with age and the boards are butted, not tongue and groove like the ones her hand is touching.

Digging into the insulation, she peals back the rolled pink material she installed and starts pushing aside the gray, shredded fiber underneath. As she digs toward the base of the gable end, she realizes that she cannot feel the joist on which the gable end ought to rest. *This wall is a façade!*

Impulse might have caused others to begin kicking at the sheathing, but not Gabby. She goes back down the ladder, gathers a hammer, pry bar, two additional flashlights and a tape measure. Before hauling all of her tools up into the attic she measures the distance from the gable end wall behind her bed back to the wall of the closet.

Once in the attic, she measures from the gable end to the spot above the closet wall—thirty-two inches shorter!

Working her way back across the joists while carrying her tools, Gabby keeps her head low for fear of hitting it on one of the rafters. All three flashlights are then positioned so they light the object of her intention. Gabby is too focused on her task to see the enormous shadows she is creating. Carefully, she begins to remove nails from what turns out to be fake studs and sheathing. As she loosens them, she realizes that the façade must have been built while lying down on the attic joists and then swung up into place before being nailed to the existing joists and rafters.

Once the wall is down, the relatively small space it conceals is visible. Cobwebs hang everywhere and the smell of stale air wafts about like a mist on a lake. All she can see are the joists with the older gray insulation between them--nothing else. *Why go to the trouble of building the fake gable end and then put nothing behind it? Maybe what ever had been hidden here has been removed. No, the nails which held the fake wall in place have been there for a long time. There were no marks on any of the wood that would result from the nails being pulled after the fake wall was built.*

For lack of a better idea, Gabby begins feeling through the insulation between the joists. Near the middle of the space her hand comes upon something wrapped in plastic.

Removing the object, she sets it aside and then begins carefully feeling around the rest of the area. Finding nothing else, she puts the façade back into place, hammering nails back into the existing holes. In her meticulous way of working, all of the tools are returned to their proper place in the workshop, the floor of the closet vacuumed and the step ladder returned down stairs before she sits down at her kitchen table to examine the package. The long, relatively thin object in the package is wrapped in just enough layers of Visqueen to prevent a "visual" identification.

Using a utility knife she cuts away the layers of black friction tape—a type of tape that electricians used forty years ago. Once the tape is cut, the package easily unrolls to reveal a rifle with a telescopic sight. Not being familiar with rifles, Gabby has no idea as to what type of gun she is holding.

Sunlight is probing the curtains of her bathroom when Gabby emerges from her second shower of the night. Exhausted from the night's work and from a total lack of sleep, she gets dressed and heads for her habitual coffee shop for a jolt of caffeine before work.

Logged on to the Wi-Fi at High Grounds she sips her latte while surfing the web trying to identify the gun. Eventually she finds a picture of the gun now in her kitchen. Wikipedia provides her with the details on what she found: Springfield .30-06, Model 1903A4 sniper rifle with a Type C stock and an M84 telescopic sight.

Chapter 7

S tanding between Galway and the window toward which he always faces, Gabby hands him a slip of paper with "M1903 30.06 rifle" written on it.

"Been busy?"

"Want to tell me anything?"

"Used one in the war."

"What unit were you in?"

"I was just a foot soldier in the war against Nazi thugs."

"Why did you own a variant of the M1903 that was used by snipers?"

"Never said I did. I saw M1903 on your paper, which is what I was first issued."

"Ever kill anyone?"

"I was an infantryman; it was a war. Any other stupid questions?"

"Why did you do such a good job of hiding it?"

"Hidin' what?"

"The 30.06."

"Who says I did?"

"You knew where to tell me to look for it."

"Doesn't mean I put it there."

"Then why leave it there?"

"I suppose I didn't want to cause a fuss."

"It was wrapped in so much Visqueen how did you know what it was?"

"This is stupid. Nurse! Leave me be."

"And why did you put in that fake wall?"

Galway wheels his chair, hits the call button and then begins heaving as if he can't catch his breath. When two CNAs arrive they bring out an oxygen tank and place a mask over the man's face. As Gabby leaves, she sees that Galway's eyes are following her, fully aware of her actions. *He's faking it.*

Standing in the hallway outside his room, Gabby looks around at her surroundings. An elderly lady with a walker is slowly making her way down the corridor toward Gabby. With her head down, concentration focused on the task of walking, she does not see Gabby. At the last second, Gabby steps aside so as not to block the woman's unwavering path. Something about the woman—stooped shoulders, print, cotton dress and fluffy pink slippers—reminds Gabby of her grandmother.

Turning away from watching the woman, Gabby is suddenly overcome with a sense of loss as she recalls the wonderful times she'd spent with "Grandma Nora" as they played endless games of rummy. But the lady in the hall also brings back the sad memories of Grandma Nora in a nursing home. The constant pungent smell of urine and the oppressive heat are all part of the sensory images Gabby recalls from the last time she saw her beloved Grandma alive.

As she comes out of the mental re-run of those bitter sweet memories, Gabby becomes aware of the smells of this place. There is a complete absence of odors from urine, antiseptics, and cleaners. This nursing home is nothing like the one she remembers.

On her way out of the nursing home, Gabby stops by the chief administrator's office, asking for a few minutes of her time.

"I am Gabriel Gordon, an attorney."

"Hello, I'm Helen Patterson." At 52, Helen stands at 5' 6", slightly overweight and graying. Her round face is always ready to smile, especially to encourage. The stress of her job with costs to control and the myriad of regulations and reports always nearing a deadline, have taken a toll on her body. On a day-to-day basis she experiences too little physical activity, too much stress, and too many pieces of birthday cake from the parties for the residents.

Gabby begins: "Mr. Galway has asked me to assist him in some of his business. As you are aware, his periods of lucidity are fleeting, so I am having some problems getting the necessary information to follow his initial requests."

"We'll be glad to assist in any way we can. Let me get his file."

When Mrs. Patterson is seated back at her desk, Gabby asks, "Do you have a Social Security number on file for him?"

"I am not sure about releasing that information."

"Mr. Galway has asked me to help him in the matter of some real estate, but he has been unable to tell me his Social Security number. When it comes to real estate, the requirements for paying any taxes that are due mean that we have to provide his number. In some ways it is more important that his full name."

"I realize what you're saying. As I look through his file, we do not have a Social Security number for him."

"Doesn't he get Medicare?"

"It appears not."

"Then who pays his fees?"

"That I do not know. All of our billing is through our corporate headquarters, which is located in Mundelein. I can contact them to get details of his financial arrangements. If he is eligible for Medicare, then they would have that information."

"I would appreciate knowing whatever they have. Here is my card. You can have them contact my office directly if it will save you the trouble."

"Oh, it's no trouble. Is there anything else?"

"Does he get many visitors? Perhaps there's some family or friends who might assist me."

"No one has been to see him since he and his wife came here. The only person he talks to on any regular basis is Max Kelstead. He's a custodian here, but he spends as much time talking to the residents as he does cleaning. That's OK with us, as most of the residents with whom he talks have no one to visit them. He provides a needed and healthy outlet for them. He thinks he's cheating us, so we let him pretend."

"Would you mind if I have a chat with Mr. Kelstead?"

"No, not at all." With that she picks up the phone to have Max paged to her office.

When he arrives, Mrs. Patterson introduces Max to Gabby and tells him that he should answer as many questions as he can about Galway. Gabby and Max walk out on to the facility's patio, taking seats on chairs facing the shady lawn as the warm air of the May afternoon floats around them.

31

Max Kelstead proves to be both quite talkative and fairly knowledgeable about Galway.

"He's told me several times about his war record. Seems he was an excellent marksman and was a sniper shooting Nazis. Got a Bronze Star medal and some other medal. Before the war ended he was transferred to the OSS. I don't know what that is. But he seemed to think I ought to be impressed by it."

"Has he ever talked about what he did after the war?"

"Not really. Says he was a private contractor of some sort. Never said what he contracted for. He married Mrs. Galway in about fifty-four, I think. She was related to some big kahuna who got John lots of work in his contractor job. Says he made lots of money, but that today he can't let people know how much he's worth."

"Where was she from?"

"The wife? Oh, Chicago, I think he said. Seems they lived there, or out in one of the suburbs for a time. He's talked about a Bus or Busy forest or something like that."

"Busse Forest Preserve?"

"Yeah, that's it. Said he went there at night from time to time, something to do with his contractor work. Sounds like it was a nice place."

"Did he ever mention other family?"

"Just his wife, and of course about her big shot father. He also said he has a sister in Florida, but she thinks he's dead and he wanted to keep it that way. Said she'd try to take his money if she knew he's still kickin'. No one else."

"Does he ever talk with any of the other residents?"

"Naw. Pretty much keeps to himself. Most folks are afraid of him. When his spells come on, he is a real son-of-witch to calm down. Except, of course, when it came to Mrs. Galway. He was always very kind and gentle with her. When she was still alive, all we had to do to calm him was to bring him back to their room. She didn't ever leave her room. Her Alzheimer's made it hard for her to move around as she became confused easily. Matter of fact, he seldom left her alone, at least not with anyone else in the room. He only left

32

her room when she was sleeping. They ate their meals in their room—he fed her, won't let anyone else. Very caring and protective. Would not leave her alone in the room even when we cleaned it. It was like he didn't want her to be around anyone if he wasn't there. She did ramble on something fierce at times."

"I neglected to ask Mrs. Patterson, but maybe you know. Does he get mail?"

"Oh, yeah. Some guy stops in once a week, usually Mondays, with a bundle of mail for him. Don't know if you noticed, but he has a paper shredder in his room. He shreds all his mail soon after he gets it, unless there is something that has to go back out. Then he hides it until Jack comes back the next week."

"Who's this Jack?"

"Uhh. Let's see. Jack…Jack…it'll come to me. A very nice black fellow. Elderly, maybe in his late seventies. Says he's been running errands for the Galways for over thirty years. Jack Bruce. That's his name. My mom went to high school with him."

"Do you know how I can get in touch with Mr. Bruce?"

"Comes in here most every Monday morning, usually about ten. I can have him get in touch with you if I see him."

"That would be wonderful. Here are two of my business cards, you can give one to Mr. Bruce when you see him and the other is for you. If you remember anything else about Mr. Galway that might help me help him, please call."

"No problem, glad to."

"Well, Mr. Kelstead thanks for your help. And, by the way, it is probably a good idea not to let Mr. Galway know we talked. He seems to get upset by the slightest things."

"Oh, don't I know it. One time, just one time, the recreation people got him to play bingo with the other guests. He won like four or five games in a row—they'd give apples or candy bars to the winners. I happened by and noticed how much stuff was piled up in front of him, so I said, 'Hey, John, you're really lucky, like a regular Lucky Luciano winning all that stuff!' He began cursing me and accusing me of being a spy. Dumped everything on the floor and wheeled out by himself. Wouldn't talk to me for weeks after that. Since then I let him do all the talking. So, this chat will definitely remain just between us."

Chapter 8

The next day Gabby sits in her office mulling over how best to secure more information on the mysterious Galway. Pending a report on a Social Security number, and she doubts if there is one, there are a couple of other avenues to pursue. However, time is not a commodity she can afford to waste. Without Internet access at home, she is restricted to the office or some public WiFi spot. That option is risky because she knows it is possible for hackers to snoop on anyone using public access spots.

Tossing down the pencil she has been twirling around her thumb, she picks up the phone and dials her secretary Samantha Greer.

Sam, as she's known to everyone, is about Gabby's age. Very bright and diligent, she is viewed skeptically by the other attorneys in the firm, but even more so by her fellow secretaries, paralegals and clerks, most of them either securely married or on their way to spinsterhood. Sam's free-swinging style, frequent changes of live-in boyfriends and growing array of tattoos are all subjects of much office gossip. Since the firm has a policy against visible tattoos, Sam has to wear long sleeved tops all year round to cover some of the gorgeous artwork that adorns her arms.

As her secretary enters the office, Gabby says, "I'm beginning an account for a John Galway. This will get billed as personal hours to me for the time being. Somewhere in the office files should be the one that Reining created when we bought Babcook Manor. Please find it as the beginning point of this project. He probably took what was the client copy with him as I've never seen it, but maybe he left both here."

"Who's this John Galway actually?"

"He's the man at The Haven who asked to speak with me. It seems he may have some claim on Babcook Manor, but he is a hard person to talk to. He suffers from dementia with only brief periods of lucidity. I need to know everything that can be found on him."

"Do you have, like, any place to start?"

"Seems to have ended up here from Chicago. Served in the US Army in World War II and then in something called the OSS. Married to a woman named Mary Alice, maiden name unknown, who died a couple years ago at The Haven. The two of them had been living there for several years before she died. She suffered from Alzheimer's disease the whole time they lived at the nursing home. That's about all I have been able to cobble together at this point."

"OK," Sam responds as she finishes writing notes. "I'll see what I can gather off the Net. Where did they actually live before moving into The Haven?"

"Babcook Manor."

"Really? Like, I grew up in Freeport, and that place was, like, considered abandoned at least twenty years ago. The story was it belonged to some Mafia dude like Al Capone or Bugsy Lawlor, or some such. Everybody avoided it 'cause there were supposed to be bodies buried all over the place."

"Well, I never found a single body the whole time I've lived and worked there. People tend to makeup stories to fill in the gaps of what they don't know. The truth is seldom as exciting as the rumors."

Chapter 9

Aweek later, Sam meets Gabby at the office's front door when Gabby, a morning latte in hand, arrives for work. "Well, actually this Galway guy does not exist. Like, the National Personnel Records Center in Saint Louis has never heard of him. The OSS was the Office of Strategic Services, the forerunner of the CIA. Of course, they do not give out any information on employees, former or otherwise. I found a death notice that was published in the *Journal Standard* for Mary Alice Galway. No funeral, private burial, no like next of kin listed. And, get this, no maiden name. Is that weird or what?"

As they reach Gabby's office, Sam continues, "Oh, and The Haven got back to us. Actually they do not have a Social Security number of John Galway. His expenses are paid monthly via direct deposit from a Chicago bank. The bills are sent to a Chicago law firm: Hoban, Boylan, Doran, and Malloy."

"Sounds like a very Irish set of senior partners. Probably big Notre Dame fans," Gabby observes wryly.

"Yeah, I bet the firm buys season football tickets by the truckload."

As Gabby sits down, Sam offers, "Oh, and get this, like according to a couple letters in the file John developed trying to sort out the deed on Babcook Manor, he, well... like, contacted this Hoban, Boylan, Doran and Malloy law firm."

"Whose name is listed as the last owner of Babcook Manor before it was deeded over to us?"

Checking her notes, Sam finally responds, "Actually, it is the Michael Joseph Flaherty Family Trust. One of the partners at Hoban, etc., a 'Sean M. Scurry, the third, Esquire,' signed the deed on behalf of the trust, which was setup in, like, nineteen-fifty-eight. Actually, Flaherty created the trust not long before his death in fifty-nine. Must've had, like, a premonition. Babcook Manor was part of the real estate owned by the trust."

"Well, I guess I better talk with this 'Sean M. Scurry, the third, Esquire.' Probably be better to talk in person rather than on the phone. Easier to read someone face-to-face."

"You think this dude's got something to actually hide?"

"I have no idea, but with the run around I'm getting from Galway, I'd rather meet this Scurry in person. Please call the Irish law firm to arrange an appointment. You have my appointment schedule with my court dates, so see if you can find a day when I would be free to drive into Chicago. I don't want to have to change any of my appointments or court dates. Thanks for all the work."

"Hey, no problem. This is like some big mystery, especially this John Galway dude. I'll put a copy of all my notes in your Galway file."

"Oh, by the way, please don't mention Galway to the Chicago lawyers. I want to see what they will admit to before I spring that information on them."

"No prob. I'll let you know when I can get that appointment. And one more thing. I know it may be none of my business, but just out of curiosity, I Googled your friend H. Elmer Barnes. His full name is Harry Elmer Barnes and he wrote over thirty books. Wikipedia said that he is a 'Holocaust Denier.' Some sort of conspiracy theory dude. Just thought I'd mention it."

Gabby is both irritated that Sam had taken it upon herself to do a rudimentary background check on Barnes and troubled by the label "Holocaust Denier." Going online Gabby finds the same Wikipedia article on Harry Elmer Barnes and quickly notes that this man died in 1968 at age 79. Obviously, this was not the same Barnes. Later Gabby tells Sam about her discovery and cautions the legal secretary about jumping to conclusions without double checking the facts, especially facts found on the Internet.

Chapter 10

Five days later Gabby is in downtown Chicago, arriving at the North Michigan Avenue address promptly for her 11:30 AM appointment with Mr. Sean M. Scurry, III. He manages to fit their meeting in between a hand ball game and some art museum board luncheon.

Walking into Scurry's office Gabby realizes at once that this is not going to go well. Scurry leers at her, running his eyes up and down the length of her body twice before she crosses the distance from the door to the chairs in front of his desk. During most of the meeting he makes no effort to conceal his ogling.

Dressed in an hand-tailored suit of expensive dark blue pinstriped fabric, Scurry also sports a heavily starched powder blue shirt—monogram on the pocket—and a gold silk necktie. Receding, sandy, red hair sits atop his oval, cheeky face that would light up like Rudolph's nose after the first glass of alcohol.

"Please have a seat," Scurry intones as he sweeps his hand toward one of the two leather chairs that sit in front of his desk. "So, Miss Gordon, how may I be of assistance?"

As Gabby sits down, she commences the meeting: "John Reining and I purchased a property in Freeport, Babcook Manor, about three and a half years ago. This firm handled the matter on behalf of the Michael Joseph Flaherty Family Trust, the owners of the property before our purchase."

"Yes, I recall the transaction." Scurry stands behind his desk, his right hand in his pants pocket constantly jingling coins. Without taking his lusting eyes off her, he uses his left hand to open the only file on top of his highly polished but very empty desk. A large banner proclaiming Notre Dame 1988 National Football Champions hangs on the wall behind him.

"My concern in coming here is that I have recently been contacted by a person who is claiming some rights to the property."

"Really? I don't see how that is possible as the property in question was in the hands of the Flaherty family since 1952, I believe. Yes, here it is in the file." At that he picks up the file and comes around the desk to sit next to her. "See here, before that, it belonged to the Catholic Diocese of Rockford." He holds out the open folder only far enough to force her to lean in towards him to see where he's pointing. Gabby is glad she's wearing a blouse that buttons all the way to her neck.

"But I think if you and I were to work very closely on this we could make sure that this person's unfounded claim is proven to be the fraud it truly is," Scurry purrs as he sits back smiling. As he crosses his legs, Gabby notices the smooth finish on the leather soles of his obviously expensive Italian shoes.

Gabby is trying to control her temper, and then realizes that she might as well use this asshole's predilections to her advantage.

"Well," she says coyly, "perhaps you can help me dig up some dirt to use against him."

"Oh, I am sure we can find something from his past that could be used to throw him off scent, so to speak."

"I would be ever so grateful if we could find a way to make this all go away without having to become entangled in a lengthy legal dispute."

"This office has many, many resources that could be put at your disposal. Your request would be my command."

"That would be most helpful. His name is John Galway."

At the mention of Galway's name Scurry blanches and slumps back in his chair, stunned into silence. As the silence gets to a length that is becoming awkward, Gabby tacks back across his bow to blast another broadside.

"I have recently finished a complete remodeling of the property with the intent of selling it and moving on to another project. So, I am concerned about any unnecessary details which might derail my plans. In addition, I have sunk considerable sums into the renovations, so I am concerned about losing my investments should this unforeseen claimant be proven legitimate."

Clearing his throat and adjusting his position in his chair, Scurry responds, "I see. How did, uh, Galway is it? How did he get in touch with you?"

"Just called my office out of the blue to tell me he had lived in the house for almost forty years. From 1963 to about 2002 if I recall correctly."

"My, that is an amazing story," Scurry demurs, again back on his feet and pacing behind his desk, his right hand in his pants pocket jingling coins. *Wonder if that's his "tell"— what he does when he's lying?* Gabby thinks to herself.

"I'm afraid we have no knowledge of such a person. If he has a claim to the house, it must pre-date the Flaherty family and the Rockford Diocese. Perhaps he is a descendant of the original owners...uhhh...the...uhhh...Babcook family." With that Scurry lays the now closed file on his desk.

"There are no living descendants of the Babcook family."

"Perhaps Mr. Babcook had some illegitimate child of which no one knew. How old is this Mr. Galway?"

"Late eighties, I'd say."

"You've met him I take it?"

"Oh, yes. I have visited him in the nursing home where he resides."

"Well, as I said," Scurry explains as he sits down behind his desk and presses his fingers together as if making a church steeple, "we have never heard of John Galway."

"You see, Mr. Scurry, I have difficulty accepting the veracity of that statement." Gabby rises to her feet and walks around to stand behind her chair to emphasize her seriousness.

"Miss Gordon, are you accusing me of giving you misinformation?"

"Disinformation would be a better descriptor." Scurry gets a puzzled look on his face; he obviously doesn't know the difference.

Gabby continues, "According to the company which owns the nursing home where Mr. Galway has lived for the past eight years, your firm has been paying his bills all that time."

"Miss Gordon, this conversation is now at an end. I cannot discuss with you legal matters outside the purview of the house you purchased from the Flaherty Family Trust." With that he presses a button on his desk phone and his secretary enters almost as if she was already on her way.

"Good day, Miss Gordon. Mrs. Hannigan will show you out."

"So, you deny that John Galway is being supported by the Flaherty Trust?"

"Goodbye Miss Gordon. Please, do drive safely on your way back to Freeport."

"Perhaps you have misunderstood my position here. I am very familiar with the laws in Illinois regarding confidentiality related to estates and trusts. What I am asking is not out of line. I am representing Mr. Galway."

Her statement seems to stop Scurry in his effort to get Gabby out of his office. But then he continues: "Please, Miss Gordon, be very, very, very careful on your way home." With that Scurry turns his back on Gabby and picks up his phone. Seeing nothing further to be gained by continuing the conversation Gabby follows the secretary out of the office.

Chapter 11

Mrs. Hannigan escorts Gabby to the elevator, but Gabby is surprised when the secretary gets on with her. Since the firm of Hoban, Boylan, Doran, and Malloy occupies the entire 76th floor of the hundred story office building, escorting a visitor "out" usually required only going as far as the elevator.

The two of them are the only people on the elevator, so once the doors close Mrs. Hannigan speaks: "I am on my way to lunch, Miss Gordon. Perhaps you should join me."

"I appreciate the offer, but I need to get back to my office."

"You might find a conversation about a mutual acquaintance a way to brighten your ride back to Freeport."

Intrigued by this, Gabby agrees. They walk to a small coffee shop only a block away. After they order, Scurry's secretary begins the conversation.

"You cannot tell anyone we talked, but you need to know that John Galway is a *nom de guerre*. For over thirty years my husband, who worked for this law firm as sort of a general go-for, drove out to Freeport twice a year with a package for John Galway. Each package contained twenty-five thousand dollars in cash—mostly twenties and fifties."

"Did the money come from the Flaherty Family Trust?" Gabby asks.

"No. The firm manages a numbered Swiss bank account for Galway. We also pay medical, nursing home and other expenses from that account as needed."

"Is there a third party between your firm and the Swiss account?"

"No. We have direct access to the account."

"Whose name is on the account?"

"Far as I know, it has only a number and then a second number that is the access code."

"Why are you helping me? This could jeopardize your job."

"Well, I know where too many of the bodies are buried around here, so to speak, for them to fire me, but the real reason has to do with my daughter, Fiona. She once worked here. Scurry's unwanted attention forced her to file a sexual harassment complaint. Since she was a first year paralegal and he was the grandson of one of the founding partners, guess who no longer works here?"

"I am sorry to hear about your daughter's problems. I sense that Scurry is a misogynist who feels he can use women as it pleases him."

"The man is the worst of slime balls. The incident which led to my daughter filing the suit happened while Scurry's wife was in the hospital giving birth to their first child. Scurry was called from the office to the hospital. On the way he spent two hours with a very expensive 'call girl,' and then called my daughter from his car when he resumed his drive to the hospital. Because he had been harassing her, she had arranged to have her calls recorded. He was using a phone paid for by the firm, so we were able to pull the log of his calls that day as part of the suit. That's how we knew he had made the call to the woman with whom he had shacked up, so to speak."

"What a sleaze. But, how do you know that John Galway is an alias?"

Gabby has no sooner asked this question than two men in nicely tailored suits sit down at the next table. Hannigan gets a perplexed look on her face as if she is trying to work out a knotty problem, but then her countenance brightens. "Check his obituary" is all she feels she can safely say at that point.

"Whose?"

"The name on the trust."

Taking the hint that Hannigan is wary of talking anymore about Galway and the trust, Gabby changes the subject to a more roundabout topic.

"So, did your husband know our mutual acquaintance well?"

"Actually, they were cousins. Their fathers were brother and brother-in-law and both worked on the Chicago and Alton Railroad. In fact, this is a little known story, but my father-in-law helped uncover a plot to kill President Theodore Roosevelt in 1903."

"Really?"

"He was a gandy dancer for the Chicago and Alton. He was working on the tracks near Bloomington when he and his crew came across a bundle of dynamite under the tracks. These were the very tracks that the President's train was scheduled to travel in a matter of a few hours."

"That is amazing. Just out of curiosity, what's a 'gandy dancer'?"

"Back in those days it was a general term for anyone who worked maintaining the tracks. I think the term is not much used these days."

The rest of the lunch is passed discussing the weather. Gabby's drive back to Freeport is uneventful, but she frequently checks her rearview mirror, Scurry's poorly-veiled threat having made her unusually cautious.

Chapter 12

That night Gabby pulls from her brief case the file which Barnes gave her. Finding the copy of the obituary of Michael Joseph Flaherty she notes some basic facts. Born in 1898 in Goshen, Indiana, he entered the U.S. Army in 1917, and was sent to France. When the war was over he traveled to Ireland where he connected with the family of his parents. Finally arriving back in the US in 1920 he settled in Chicago where he was soon owner and manager of a soft drink distribution company. The obituary implied that he turned that small beginning into a financial empire. He became a generous patron of charities and the Chicago Archdiocese. He married, had one daughter and two sons. The obit gave no further information on the sons, but it stated that he was survived by his wife and his daughter—"Mrs. Sean Michael (Mary Alice) Fallon of Bridgeport."

The next morning Sam is set to work tracking down Sean Michael Fallon's military service records. Pending further information from Sam's research, Gabby decides to take a day to search for more information on Flaherty. A call to Barnes reveals the following:

"Where did you obtain the copy of Flaherty's obit?" Gabby queries.

"My dear, the library at Northern Illinois University has back copies of all Chicago newspapers on microfilm as well as complete indices for each."

After she gets off the phone, Gabby chuckles at Barnes's precise terminology. Only someone like Barnes would use the formal plural of "index" – "indices" instead of the more commonly used "indexes."

Finding information on Flaherty is easy as he had lots of press at the time of his death. While the obit Barnes found is pretty non-committal on Flaherty's "business" efforts, the news stories at the time of his death are filled with detailed speculation, especially about providing money and guns to outlawed groups in Ireland. While it makes for fascinating reading, Gabby begins to feel that Flaherty is a blind alley.

Switching to Mary Alice Flaherty, a notice of her engagement to Sean Michael Fallon was easily located. His occupation is listed as a "business consultant." The article on the wedding is accompanied by a photo of the newlyweds, showing a young man who could be Galway, but Gabby would be hard pressed to say for sure they are one in the same. The article provides lots of information in the way of descriptions of the bridal gown and other such information usually supplied in lavish detain for the wedding of anyone from a wealthy family "back in the day." The final sentence notes that the couple will honeymoon in Ireland in the county of her ancestors—Galway.

Chapter 13

There is no chapter 13.

Chapter 14

When Jack Bruce calls the office to setup an appointment, Gabby is curious as to how much information he will be able or willing to divulge. Later, as she greets him in the waiting room, Gabby notes that he is in his mid to late seventies. A tall, slim man with graying temples, he has large hands and a genuine smile. Gabby escorts Bruce back to her office, offering him a seat and something to drink.

"No, thank you. Mr. Kelstead said you wanted to see me. Something about Mr. Galway?"

"Yes, I have been hired by Mr. Galway to sort out a problem with some property he owns, but his dementia is making it hard to get the facts straight. I hope you can help."

"Well, I don't know. Mr. Galway has been pretty good to me and he has warned me many times not to talk to anyone about what I do for him."

"I understand, so please do not tell me anything you feel will violate his trust in you. How long have you worked for him?"

"Pretty near thirty-one years. I used to work at Lee's Grocery Store making deliveries, and one of the places I delivered to was where Mr. and Mrs. Galway lived. They were always very generous tippers, but demanded that I not talk to anyone about coming to their place."

"I do not want to be rude, Mr. Bruce, but how generous were they?"

"Just an extra five bucks at first, but soon, after they felt comfortable with me, it was twenty, then fifty. Then they asked me to set up a Post Office box for them and bring them their mail once a week. They did not like having their mail delivered to the house."

"Babcook Manor?"

"Yes. When Lee's closed I lost my job and Mr. and Mrs. Galway were hunting for someone to bring them food

49

each week. So they started paying me to do their grocery shopping and continue the mail. I'd bring their mail on Monday morning's and they'd give me a shopping list and cash. After I got everything on the list, I'd bring it back and they would pay me for my work. Before Mrs. Galway got sick and they moved to the nursing home, they were paying me $200 per week."

"They seem very generous. So, they had a Post Office box. Did you ever look at where some of their mail came from?"

"To be honest, I felt that would be prying. Besides, I figured that they must be hiding from someone, so I figured the less I knew the safer I'd be. Seemed odd though."

"What seemed odd?"

"They were such nice folks and all, and so generous. To think that they must have done something bad didn't seem to rightly fit. If you know what I mean."

"I do, Mr. Bruce. Did they ever get any strange packages?"

"Oh, they got many packages, but none seemed out of the ordinary. Mr. Galway got books all the time. Belonged to several of those book-of-the-month kinda things and got many, many packages from them. They were clearly marked in big letters on the outside that they were books, so I couldn't help but notice that.

"Funny thing about all those books was that about once a year he'd have me haul bunches of them to the public library as donations. I figured he'd read a book and then give it away. Pretty generous, if you ask me."

"Anything else you noticed about their mail?"

"On several occasions there were large envelopes from some bank in Switzerland. I only noticed that because I had to sign for them and then Mr. Galway had to send back letters that needed to be signed for on their end. I had no idea how expensive it was to send something like that to a foreign country."

"Well, Mr. Bruce, you have been most helpful. Thank you for taking the time to stop by. And, by the way it may be best if Mr. Galway does not know we talked. He gets strange ideas and I don't want to upset him needlessly."

At this statement, Jack Bruce gets a strange look on his face and Gabby realizes that she has made him suspicious. *He will tell Galway the first chance he gets.*

Chapter 15

L et's just get to the purpose of your visit," snarls Galway after him and Gabby chit-chat for a few minutes.

"OK, what's your real name?"

"Why? Don't like the one I got?"

"There is no Social Security number for John Galway."

"I guess I forgot to get one."

"And the United States Army has never heard of a John Galway who fits your description."

"There were over ten million of us in durin' the war. I can imagine there are more than a few who fell through the cracks."

"You seem to have fallen through quite a few cracks. Just out of curiosity, how did you and your wife get groceries all those years you supposedly lived in the basement and never went outside?"

"Lee's grocery store delivered. After they went out of business, we hired a guy to do shoppin' for us."

"Jack Bruce?"

"You've been busy."

"No telephone?"

"Didn't have anyone to call and didn't want anyone callin' us."

"No TV?"

"Listened to the radio. Great invention that NPR. Got tired of that talk radio and the hip-hop shit they play on most stations."

"No car, no driver's license, no voter registration. You've led a hardscrabble life?"

"Car was stolen and never got it back. No car after that so why have a license? Votin' only makes the politicians think they're important. And we were never much for playin' board games."

"You've got an answer for everything. So tell me, MISTER GALWAY, what's your relationship with Hoban, Boylan, Doran, and Malloy?" That one catches him off guard.

52

"Surprised I found that? Shouldn't be, The Haven does have a record of where they send the bill each month for your stay in their facility. The name Michael Joseph Flaherty mean anything to you?"

"Suppose it does and suppose I do have a business arrangement with Hoban, Boylan, Doran, and Malloy. None of these 'supposes' have a thing to do with the real issues that ought to concern ya and Babcook."

"Just what should concern me about that house, Mister Galway?"

"Facts related to the house. You're busy chasin' shadows of facts, but the important ones have yet to be uncovered."

"Well, when you get it in your head to talk to me on something approaching a level of the truth, you've got my number." With that Gabby rises from her seat and heads for the door, but Galway waves her back.

After a long pause as he appears to weigh his next words, he speaks, "Mary and me lived in that house, the basement, for more years than I care to count. I don't know how it was when ya first looked at it, but we kept the place spotless. There was no furniture in any rooms 'cept the basement where we lived. Everyday we'd dust and sweep and keep everything tidy in the entire house. I guess that was just the way we was made. But, missy, there are things about that house that need to be known before ya try to sell to someone who might not understand all that's involved."

"Then why are you being so opaque about what I need to know?"

"Please cut an old man some slack as I try to work through this. And one last thing. Ya know anythin' about Charlie Guiteau's Message?"

53

Chapter 16

S am tells Gabby that Charles Guiteau was a Freeport resident who assassinated some president and that his house on Galena Avenue has sat empty "for, like eons 'cause its haunted."

In need of a more factual background Gabby makes an appointment to meet with Barnes at his home that evening. Barnes lives in a brick two story house only a few minutes' walk from the museum. The unique house has a round tower-like structure that encloses the front door.

Barnes greets Gabby at the door, a short, pointy-eared dog at his heels.

"Good evening, Gabriel. Don't mind Alfred Thayer; he'll just lick you to death."

"What type of dog?"

"Pembroke Welsh Corgi. Named Alfred Thayer Mahan."

"I see," Gabby responds with raised eyebrows.

"Oh, you see, my dear, he's named for the man about whom I wrote my doctoral dissertation. I argued that Mahan's theories on naval power were the roots of the military-industrial complex. But that's ancient history now, though Alfred got stuck with the moniker."

"So, how did a naval historian end up as a rare book curator at the Smithsonian?"

"Uhhh. Well, that was an accident of names. As I was finishing my doctoral work and looking for a job teaching at a university, I discovered there was another historian with the same name—first, last and middle. Only this Dr. Barnes was some sort of crackpot who denied that the Holocaust had ever happened. Needless to say, no respectable college or university was willing to hire someone with the same name as that man, even though he died before I finished graduate school. Through the help of my dissertation committee chair, I was able to land a spot at the Smithsonian.

"Knowing that I would have great trouble publishing any work in the field of naval and World War II history, which were my areas of study, I made the decision to devote my career to the collection and conservation of rare books."

"That must have been a disappointment."

"It had its rewards, and I became very content with my career. Now, let me get the kettle on while you have a seat."

Barnes' living room is one large library with every speck of wall space covered with bookshelves. Gabby can also see shelves filled with books running down the hallway to the kitchen. What she senses is that Barnes lives the life of an intellectual whose idle hours are spent with classical music, the Sunday *New York Times* and a delight in the joy of ideas. Yet Gabby also senses that he has the grace to make anyone feel at ease.

As her gaze roams around the, room she notices a portrait of a very attractive woman on the fireplace mantle. The formal photo appears to have been taken when the woman was in her twenties.

"That's Elsa," Barnes says as he re-enters the room and follows Gabby's gaze to the photo on the mantle. "We were married for thirty-nine years. She was a great lover of Wagner; her opera tastes were deeper than mine, as I prefer Verdi and Puccini. Elsa was a gifted linguist who taught German at Georgetown University. She was the 'reward' that came with my decision to stay in rare books. We met while I was working on a couple of books by German authors and she was serving as a consultant on the project.

"She passed away just before we were to retire. We intended to spend our 'golden years' in world travel. We had no children and were both without siblings. But when she died I simply moved back to Freeport since I had no place else to go; our Georgetown home was too full of memories for me to remain there."

"I'm sorry for your loss."

"Thank you." With that Barnes grows quiet as he busies himself with the tea in an effort to cover for his emotions. Gabby watches as Barnes spoons lose tea leaves from a tin into a tea pot and then pours in hot water from a second pot. The tin is a beautiful aqua blue with a purple ban around the middle. Gold lettering indicates the "Classic Earl Grey Tea" is from Fortnum and Mason. Picking up the colorful tin, Gabby sees in small print, "By Appointment to Her Majesty Queen Elizabeth II."

As Barnes pours the steeped tea into cups already containing milk, he says, "I purchase my tea from an on-line source that imports in from the U.K. One lump or two, my dear?"

When they both have full cups and are seated, he begins, "Now, to the reason for your visit. Charles Guiteau was born into a rather wealthy and prominent local family. His half-sister Flora was one of the co-founders of the local chapter of the League of Women Voters. The Guiteaus were socially connected to the family of Jane Addams, as well as the Henney, Rawleigh and Babcook families. But ole Charlie suffered from an ill-defined mental defect. Some said that most of his siblings were also a couple degrees off plumb, but I've never seen any documented proof of that. Seems Charlie went off to Oneida, New York from whence his family had migrated to Freeport in the first place. In Oneida he joined a utopian society that practiced some form of free love. Despite his visions of becoming the Lothario of the sect, Charlie's huggermugger mental condition caused the women in that 'brave new world' to shun him. Unable to partake of the advertised free love, he left in a great huff to seek an appointment from the new administration in Washington.

"His services were declined by the politicos, so in 1881 Charlie shot President Garfield, claiming that the president had promised him a patronage job and then reneged. Of course, Charlie was put on trial for murder, as Garfield eventually died of the gunshot. More recent examinations of the case have shown an iatrogenic root cause of death in that Garfield's doctors did more harm than Charlie's bullet. But in 1882 Charlie was found guilty and hanged."

"What about that house on Galena that belonged to him?"

"Well, that house belonged to Charles' uncle, not to Charles or his father. It has been empty for many, many decades. Someone or other from time to time will get the idea about rehabilitating it for use as a museum or such, but there is limited interest for such a project and even less funding. Neighborhood Services bought it a few years ago and got a grant to replace the roof and stabilize the floors, but now it still sits empty as no one can find a use for it that makes the cost of a restoration worthwhile. You see, it has no space for patron parking, off street or on, and for it to be of any use one would have to purchase one of the houses next door and raze it."

"So, what can you tell me about the so-called 'Charles Guiteau Message'?"

"With whom have you been talking? By the way, you're not thinking of buying the derelict as your next rehab project, are you?"

"No, I just heard something mentioned in passing about the message and Guiteau, so here I am."

"Well, there are two versions of the story about the Guiteau Message. One is that Charlie wrote a short piece of doggerel and arranged for the hangman to release the trapdoor from under Charlie's feet when Charlie dropped the piece of paper. That seems to have some basis in fact. The other story is that Charlie had written some manifesto about religious intolerance and that its secret burial place was contained on a slip of paper that Charlie hid behind one of the fireplace mantels in his uncle's house."

"Anyone ever look for it?"

"Oh, yes, my dear. The last time was when they were working on the house a couple years back. There was a committee of us who got to go through the house once the floors were deemed safe. We never found a thing. Didn't expect to, really. The problem with the 'message behind the fireplace' story is that in order for the note about the location of his treatises to have been placed there by Charlie, he would have to have written it before he left Freeport for Oneida. That was long before Garfield was elected president and long before Charlie became agitated over religion. The whole thing is bunk. Urban myths we call them today. Still, in this country we've made a cottage industry out of conspiracy theories and such nonsense. Another cup of tea, my dear?"

Chapter 17

B ack home that night, Gabby ponders what she now knows about Guiteau and the supposed message. Two paths seem to lie before her: one, since the message story has been debunked, then Galway's reference to it is just another lie from someone who is very good at prevarication; or two, Galway does not know the story is untrue so he wants to use its basic facts to steer Gabby toward something else hidden in Babcook Manor. The more Gabby tries to reason her way through it, the more she realizes that it does not matter if Galway knows the truth of the story. He can still use it as a clue.

It is after 9 PM when Gabby decides to begin hunting for a "message hidden behind a mantel." As she approaches the back of the manor from the garage she notices that the back door of the kitchen is ajar. For a moment she hesitates on to what to do. She does not remember leaving the door open, and it has been a couple days since she was inside the house. Deciding on a plan, Gabby walks over to the house where she closes and locks the door. Then she retraces her steps back to the garage to retrieve a flashlight, tool belt, and, in a last minute addition, her hand gun.

When she gets back to the house, the back door is again standing open. Obviously an intruder was inside when she locked the door. Deducing that the house is now empty, Gabby goes inside, locking the door behind her. After turning on all the lights in the house from the master control panel near that same door, she begins a systematic search of the premises. The flashlight is in her back pocket, but her gun is at the ready in her right hand. It will be later, when she pauses long enough to think through her actions, that she becomes nervous over the ramifications of the situation and how casually she decided to go through the house on her own.

Finding nothing untoward in her search, Gabby sticks the gun in her jeans at the small of her back. Then she turns her attention to the fireplace mantel in the living room. It is a marble fixture that is cemented in place from when the house was built. The final coat of plaster on the walls surrounding the fireplace was put on after the installation of the whole fixture, so there are no openings which would have allowed for a slip of paper to be inserted.

She is about to move on to another fireplace—the house has four—when it occurs to her that whoever concocted the Guiteau/mantle story may not have known what constituted a mantle on a fireplace. Walking back to the kitchen she retrieves a set of vinyl gloves from a drawer and puts them on as she returns to the living room. Gabby then examines the fire box and as far up the flue as she can see with her flashlight. Again finding nothing she moves on.

The mantel in the master bedroom is of the same type of construction as the one in the living room so it is also tightly fitted into its plaster wall. P.W.'s study has a fireplace, but it is all brick. A careful examination shows that there are no lose bricks, no lose mortar, and more importantly, no mantle. Frustrated that she has now spent an hour inspecting fireplaces, she half-heartedly makes her way down to the basement, where a rustic fireplace is located in the room where Galway and his wife supposedly lived for so many years.

The mantel there is made from a large plank of pine, some eight feet long, six inches thick and two feet deep. It is set on top of brick extensions on both wings of the fireplace. At first glance the mantel appears to have been tightly abutted to the surrounding surfaces on all sides. However, while running her fingers along the top of the back edge, she feels a gap about a foot from the right end. Using her flashlight she peers into the gap. To her surprise there seems to be something white down in the crack. Using a pair of needle-nosed pliers from her tool belt she pulls out a folded piece of paper.

Before she can unfold it, Gabby jumps at the sound of one someone rattling the kitchen's back door. She stands in silence for almost five minutes, expecting at any second to hear footsteps on the floor above. When no sounds come, she slowly ascends back to the kitchen. The bitter taste of iron in her mouth tells her that adrenal is in her blood stream as she expects at any moment to come face-to-face with an intruder.

Peering around the corner from the hallway into the kitchen, she cannot see anyone outside the massive windows that look out on the patio from the kitchen and family room. Going over to the door, gun again in her right hand, she finds that the door is closed and locked, just as she left it.

Leaving on all of the lights in the house, she exits through that same kitchen door, again locking it behind her. With the gun at the ready, she walks across the drive to the side door of the garage. That door is locked, also just as she left it. Letting herself in, she relocks the door and then checks to make sure that the back door of the garage is also locked. She flips the circuit breaker to turn off on the electric garage door openers before going upstairs to her apartment. Once there she locks the door at the top of the stairway, something she has never done since moving in three years ago.

Back in the small kitchen of her apartment, she sits down to examine the paper, her gun lying on the table close at hand. The paper is an eight by ten piece of tracing paper that has been folded in half and then again in thirds. On the paper are three circles spaced in what seems to be a random pattern. Lines from each circle run out to intersect in one corner of the page. Along each line is a number, each number different from the others. Where the lines meet is the number five. All of the circles and lines were made with a pencil and there are pencil lead/finger smudges here and there on the page.

Turning the diagram this way and that, she can make no sense of it. Realizing that it is past midnight, Gabby places the "message" in a Ziploc bag, seals it and puts it between the two pizzas in the freezer of her refrigerator. Before going into her bedroom she sits down with the phone book, looks up the number of a home security alarm company and makes note of it so she can call it first thing in the morning.

Sleep never comes that night, just as it has managed to elude her for most nights since she was first summoned to the room of John Galway. All of the information she has accumulated chases itself around in her brain, only to be interrupted from time to time with the image of that open kitchen door. She does not replace her gun in its safe until she is ready to leave for work the next morning.

Chapter 18

The home security rep agrees to meet Gabby at Babcook Manor the afternoon after the open kitchen door incident. He is to examine the buildings and draw up a plan and an estimate for the installation of an alarm system. Gabby tells the rep that she wants a system that is completely independent of any phone lines and has a battery backup in the event of a power failure.

When Gabby gets home that afternoon the sun is still far above the horizon on an early June day, the sales rep is there as agreed. He is walking around the house and the grounds, drawing a map with a device that uses GPS and lasers to measure distances and plot them on a hand-held mini-computer.

As Gabby lets the man into the house, a car is pulling up the quarter-mile long driveway. Not recognizing the older-model Volvo station wagon, Gabby walks out to meet the driver as he gets out. In his early thirties with dark hair, he stands about six feet tall with a well maintained body--wide shoulders narrowing at the hips sculpted muscles showing from his short-sleeved shirt—he obviously works out.

"Is there something you wanted?" Gabby asks.

"Hi, I'm Glenn Logan. I am with Hunter, Jameson, Baylor and Anna Architects and Planners from Madison. Here is my card." As he hands the card to Gabby he steps around her to look at the house. "My, my, my—you're even more of a beauty than I could have imagined."

"I beg your pardon."

"Sorry, I was speaking to the house."

"Oh. Well, thank you, I guess. I'm the owner."

"How long have you had the house?"

"Little over three years."

"She's in great shape on the outside. How's the interior?"

"Just as good. Are you interested in buying? I'm just getting ready to put it on the market."

"Oh, I'd love to own something like this, but what's a single guy going to do with something this size?"

"Is there something you wanted in particular?"

"Oh, I'm sorry. I get so carried away looking at vintage homes I sometimes forget my manners," Glenn explains as he keeps his eyes on Babcook. "Many years ago my firm acquired the business of the architect who designed this house. His name was Ethan Lucas. I am an architect specializing in historic restorations, but my hobby is also historic homes. For the past year, I have been combing through my company's oldest files to find designs that are interesting. Then I use vacation days or weekends to see if I can find them. When I find one still standing I like to take pictures to update our files and satisfy my history bug."

"I see. Well this house has just undergone a complete renovation."

"What contractor did you use? They did a fantastic job."

"I did the work myself."

At that, Glenn wheels around from the house and for the first time casts an appreciative eye on Gabby. A smile spreads across his face as he stares. Feeling the need to break the awkwardness of the moment by extending her hand while saying, "Hi, I'm Gabriel Gordon."

"Are you a contractor?"

"No, I'm an attorney. Rehabbing old houses is my hobby. This is my second project."

"So, you're not going to live in it?"

"No, way too much house for just me. I've been living in the apartment above the garage for the past three years while I work on the house weekends and such. Just getting ready to put the house on the market and start looking for a new project."

"You might be interested in what I have." He heads back to his car from which he pulls out a roll of blueprints. "This is a copy made from the architect's original plans."

"Holy moly petoli!" Gabby exclaims as she examines the plans.

"I beg your pardon?"

"Old family expression. But these plans, I would have given anything for these a couple of years ago. Tracing the wiring was a real hassle, and determining where some of the structural members were located was also a pain."

"Did you demolish the original plaster, Miss Gordon?"

"Call me Gabby. No, not on the first floor. The second floor bedrooms were very large but with no closets and only one full bath for the entire house. So I took the lath and plaster out and moved walls to create one full bath for every two bedrooms. I also added closets in each. If I had taken the walls down to the studs on the first floor, then rewiring would have been simpler. But I wanted to retain as much of the original lath and plaster as possible. It was in remarkably good condition for the age of the house, so preserving it was a priority."

"So, Gabby, please call me Glenn, do you mind if I take a look around?"

With that they set off to explore with the blueprints in hand. The presence of the alarm company rep completely escapes Gabby's mind until he finds her to say he's finished with his survey and will be in touch with an estimate.

Glenn is impressed with the way Gabby has re-purposed the east wing of the house, expanding P.W.'s office into a more modern space with built-in bookcases and desk and also creating an adjacent conference room out of what had been the maid's quarters.

"This arrangement would make it a snap to work from home or run a business out of here. And I gotta admit that the huge bronze 'B' on the front of the house is impressive. I would think any future owner would want to keep it as I am sure it's a landmark in town."

"Well, it may look impressive, but it was one son-of-a-witch to polish back to its original shine. I lost track of how many cans of Brasso I used, standing on a scaffold and running an electric buffer," Gabby moans as she shakes her head.

"Why didn't you take it down? It would have been a lot easier to polish."

"The brackets holding it are so rusted that I figured I'd have to have new ones made if I took it down. And not only did it take hours and hours to get the darn thing shining, it actually stood out clearer when it had the dark patina. Now that it's polished it can be hard to notice at times against the light-colored bricks."

After almost two hours in and around the house, Glenn starts talking about needing to get on the road back to Madison. With a few false starts at asking the right question without seeming to ask the direct question, the two agree to have dinner. Gabby takes Glenn to Cannova's where they share a bottle of Chianti over simple but excellent pasta with marinara. All the while they discuss the designs of late nineteenth and early twentieth century homes.

When they get back to the Manor there is again some awkwardness as each contemplates making some suggestion about furthering their relationship. Each is obviously attracted to the other, but both think better of it, or maybe it is the fact that both are generally shy about moving relationships to another level, given their past marital disasters. In the end, Glenn leaves Gabby with his cell number and the full set of plans he brought. In addition they agree to go on a road trip next Saturday to seek another house on Glenn's list.

After Glenn leaves, Gabby realizes that she has spent over six hours without once thinking about Galway and his machinations. They have been wonderful, almost magical hours. Glenn is also divorced and Gabby can feel that he has some hesitancy about getting into a relationship too quickly. That mirrors her feelings. *That caution is good* she tells herself as she gets into bed, the wine having further relaxed her spirits.

Her hopes for a peaceful rest are unmet as the delightful evening with Glenn brings back unwanted and painful memories. Through half dream and partially conscious memory, Gabby recalls the events three years ago that led to the dissolution of her marriage. As she tosses and turns the past events roll through her mind like a movie.

#   #   #

The usual quiet of the Weston and Sanderson Law Offices was shattered by two very loud door slams followed by the crash of a falling file cabinet hitting a desk and then the floor. Like ground squirrels, the heads of clerks and secretaries poked up above the walls of their cubicles as Gabby emerged from her office. All were looking toward the source of the sound— Tom's office.

Hector Weston, the portly octogenarian senior partner of the firm came out of his office, down in the far corner of the complex from Gabby's. He motioned for Gabby to come his way via the far side of the full-floor suite which W&S occupied, the middle area being the habitat of the ground squirrels.

Once Gabby was in Hector's office, he closed the door, locked it and motioned her to a seat at his conference table. The locking of the door further unnerved her as the shock of "bam, bam, thud, thud" still echoed in her mind.

"Perhaps it is not in my purview to tell you this, but I feel that in the interest of your own safety I need to do so," began Hector at his usual leisurely pace.

"We have just offered Tom the chance to resign— immediately—or face dismissal for cause. As you heard, he is not happy about the firm's ultimatum, and as of this moment, I have no idea which way he will choose to leave. Either way, today is his last day with Weston and Sanderson."

"Why? What's happened?" stammered Gabby in confusion.

"It is unfortunate that I have to tell you, but you need to hear it from someone and I am not sure you will get a complete story from Tom. The Chief Circuit Judge has informed us that she has formally notified Tom that he will be referred to the Illinois Bar Association for discipline."

"What? How can that be? What's he done?"

"Over the past year Tom has been soliciting sex from some of the women he has represented in divorce cases. The Chief Judge has received a complaint from one of the women, who apparently has decided to make the charges because she sees herself as the proverbial 'woman scorned,' as she had come to believe that she and Tom would marry once her divorce was finalized. Instead Tom began a relationship with a current client resulting in 'the telling of tales out of school' so to speak."

"Oh, my God! This can't be true. I've got to talk to Tom. There has to be a misunderstanding," Gabby whispered as she began to stand.

Hector gently put his hand on her arm, signaling her to remain a bit longer. "Gabriel, there may be little to be gained by that course of action at the present time. Tom has not denied the charges, but is angry that his behavior, which he seems to feel is no one else's business, has been called into question, let alone called to our attention. We have been aware of his propensities for almost six months, hours he billed for these cases being substantially less than the amount of time he seemed to have been devoting to them. And there were his evening meetings with clients here in the office."

"Why was I never informed?"

"We were not absolutely certain of the facts until now. The high esteem in which everyone in our firm holds you has caused us to shield you from our fears. Perhaps we were remiss in doing so, as you by right ought to have been informed, but in truth, none of us had the heart to tell you. Hoping that it would all die away, or that Tom would extricate himself both from your marriage and the firm before it came to light, we hesitated for too long. Please forgive us for that. It was done in what we thought was your best interest."

"Is there sufficient evidence to sustain the charge?" Gabby's argumentative instincts kicked into gear at this point.

"Regrettably, it would seem so. I am sure that Judge Crockett would not have decided to push this issue to the State Bar without the necessary evidence to back the charges. She is not given to flights of fancy and is known to be intolerant of any form of sexual hijinks."

Deflated again, Gabby responded, "I see your point, and I can appreciate the desire of the firm to distance itself from having one of its associates hauled up on ethics charges."

She fell into silence as the extent of Tom's infidelity became fully realized.

Hector interrupted her reverie, "Do you have a place to spend the night? We do not think it in your best interest to go home with him tonight. I have never seen him so angry, and I would not want you in some un-fortuitous situation ..."

Hectors voice tailed off as Gabby gazed out the window at a growing compendium of thunder heads in the western sky. *This only happens in novels*, she mused in her mind as the dissolution of her marriage and the pending thunder storm seemed to coincide. Her thoughts were broken by a gentle knock on Hector's door.

"Who is it?" the elder attorney queried.

"Kaelyn, Mr. Weston. May I enter?"

"One moment, please," Hector responded as he hefted his considerable bulk from his chair to go unlock the door.

Kaelyn Levins, the matronly secretary to Hector Weston, poked her head in the door. "He left a few minutes ago, taking a file box of his personal items. Left a mess for Anita what with the contents of the file box having been tossed all around his office in addition to the dumped file cabinet."

"Let's not worry about that now, Miss Levins. It can all be straightened out in due course. Do call Freeport Lock Company to have the office's outer locks changed and new keys distributed to staff before the end of day. Also, please call the alarm company and have Mr. Reining's code voided."

"Yes, sir. Gabby, I am sorry, oh, so sorry."

"Thank you for the kindness," was all that Gabby could think to reply. With that Kaelyn left, silently closing the door behind her.

"Where will you go tonight?"

"I don't know, really," Gabby responded dreamily as she resumed staring out the window. "I am not convinced that Tom is a threat to me. I have seen, on rare occasions, his temper, but it was never directed at a person, usually a stubborn nail or a very tight radiator pipe, and it never lasted for more than a couple minutes."

"Are you still living in an apartment?"

Gabby nodded her head. "Babcook Manor is not yet habitable. We've only just begun the rehab. I suppose I need to retain an attorney as there'll be a divorce to navigate."

"That is a good supposition for you to make. Pick anyone here in the firm to represent you. *Pro bono* would be operative here."

"Seems odd, doesn't it? This morning we left the apartment as a seemingly happily married couple. Now it's over. How could there be any trust left? Maybe I trusted too much all along. Never suspected, not even with all of his night-time appointments. But they say the wife is always the last to know. In this case, I guess the common wisdom is correct."

Hector was content to allow Gabby to talk on as she processed her thoughts and emotions. In a state of shock, her thoughts became random, almost as if she was detached from the situation.

"Have you ever considered that the words 'promise' and 'promiscuous' share the same first six letters? Ha!" Gabby fell silent again. After a few more minutes of silent thought, she began again:

"Reminds me of the time when I was working in a book store in college. One of the other clerks, a naïve, middle-aged woman who seemed to lack any formal education and who spent all of her time reading what us college kids jokingly referred to as 'heaving bosoms romance novels,' discovered that her husband had been cheating on her. In telling her fellow employees about the situation, one of the other workers jokingly suggested that she needed to hire a 'shyster lawyer' as a means of getting revenge. Later that day she approached me with the phone book opened the yellow pages and asked me how to spell 'shyster.' We all thought it was great fun at the time, but now I'm left wondering if I don't need one."

"Well, we have all represented clients in divorce cases that were acrimonious, to say the least," Hector offered in a gentle voice, "but I have yet to see one case where the injured party felt better when it was all over if the other party had been thrashed in the settlement. Revenge may be a dish best served cold, but it seldom provides a meal of any lasting satisfaction. Retribution is best left in the hands of God."

"You're right. At least intellectually I can see the merit of your point. Still there would be some satisfaction in taking him apart in a courtroom. But to do that I'd need to represent myself and we both know the old adage about the person who is her own attorney."

"Yes, a fool for a client. Best leave that to someone with a little professional distance, and if you feel that none of us here can provide that distance, I am sure any attorney in town would be honored to have you seek his or her assistance."

Turning her gaze toward the door as she rose, Gabby expressed her appreciation to Hector for his concern and advice. As she walked back to her office, she passed Tom's, where the door is thankfully closed.

Sitting in her own office gazing off at the angry council of a thunder storm that continued to accumulate in the west, she tried to digest the last thirty minutes—a half hour that altered the course of her life as surely as a fatal car wreck.

Later she would marvel at the lack of anger she felt toward Tom. She came to feel that somehow she had always known things would end like this. It was only a matter of time before they reached a point where their relationship had run its course. Building a marriage solely on a mutual interest in house renovation proved to be the proverbial castle built in the sky. But at this moment all that seemed to occupy her mind though was sorting out the legal mess of Babcook Manor.

Their cars were still titled in their own names and they owned no other property jointly but some furniture and tools. *TOOLS! Ah, now "there's the rub!"* As the renovation on the Italianate-style house progressed, they'd invested in an expensive miter saw; a radial arm saw; a hefty joiner; and a rather substantial lathe. In addition, there were hand-held tools: circular saws, drills, and jig saws. Sorting all that out might be contentious.

For almost an hour Gabby's mind roiled with speculation about potential points of contention in a divorce.

Finally, she was interrupted when Sam stuck her head in the door.

"You alright?"

"Yeah. As right as one can be after being kicked in the stomach," Gabby responded through a weak smile.

"Gabby, I did not know about any of Tom's dickin'…sorry, I mean, like fooling around until this all blew up," Sam said as she closed the door and moved to a seat. "Apparently the old biddies who try to control the office gossip decided that if they told me then I would tell you. I wish I could have given you a head's up."

"That's okay; I probably would have denied it. Just out of curiosity, did you…"

"Gabby, no, no, no, no. I would never…"

"Sam, that's not what I meant. I am just curious about whether Tom ever hit on you or if you picked up any vibes that he was … looking?"

"No. Not a clue. Maybe he was at least smart enough not to go sniffing too close to home."

They sat there for a few minutes in silence but then Gabby picked up the photo of Tom that sat on the cadenza behind her desk and threw it across the room. It smashed into shards of glass and splinters of wood. "That selfish piece of chicken shit. If I had the no-good, dirty rotten, unmitigated bastard here I'd fix it so the only permanent job he could get would be singing in the Vienna Boys Choir!"

"That's the spirit, girlfriend. Now, like we need to go out for drinks to let you drown in the memories of the jerk. It'll do you good to get some of it out of your system."

"I'm game. It's almost five, so let us sally forth in search of the perfect cabernet. Where do you want to go?"

"Eilert's is a good spot. They, like have appetizers that will help slow the effects of the booze as we skewer the dog with our wit and profanity!"

Ensconced in a back corner of the bar, Gabby was regaled with tales of Sam's on-going battles with the opposite sex—Sam's effort to keep Gabby from becoming too focused on her own troubles.

"… So Al asked me to, like move in with him, but it turned out the son of a bitch actually was married and wanted me to actually move in with him AND his wife."

"Dear God. What did you do?"

"So, I stole his cell phone and when his wife called, I told her that he had just left but had left his cell laying there. Then I said there was a group of us celebrating his marriage and, I added just for spite that when he left here he and his new bride were, like going on their honeymoon."

"You've got to be kidding," Gabby said as she doubled over in laughter.

"When he gets home that night a battle royal ensues. Neighbors, like call the cops and both end up like in jail. Him for assaulting her and her for assaulting a police officer who tried to stop her from going after him with one of his hunting knives."

"Remind me never to piss you off, girlfriend."

After they drink several glasses of wine and Gabby was feeling no pain Sam calls a cab to take them both home.

In a state of numbness, both from the wine and the emotional body blows she'd received, Gabby entered her apartment, finding that Tom had been there and gone. His clothes were gone, but the few items of furniture they had acquired were there, along with all of the tools. He left his keys to both the apartment and Babcook Manor on the kitchen counter, along with his office keys.

So, Gabby's mind summed, *this is what's left of three years' of marriage: a couple sets of keys.* She sat down and fought tears. When she was little, Daddy always told her that carpenters don't cry. That night, however, Gabby was not a carpenter; she was hurt and needed to let her emotions escape, though they were coming out in ways she had long been told were signs of weakness.

Fighting the tears, Gabby went down to the garage where their tools were stored. She cleared a work space, hooked up the radial arm saw, and began working on a plank. Two hours later she has reduced the 12 foot long 2" by 10" board to a complete pile of sawdust. Methodically she made ½-

inch deep cuts on one side—the cuts being so close together that nothing is left between each cut. Then she flipped the plank over and did the same to the other side. What remained was a board 12 feet long and three quarters of an inch thick, which she again went over with the saw, this time eliminating the board completely. *I love the smell of sawdust* went through her mind as each pull on the saw removed another fraction of an inch of Tom's skull.

Later she found a Post-it note on the grandfather clock that had been a gift from Tom's father. It proclaimed that he would contact her about picking it up at some later time. None of the tools were similarly tagged. There is neither a note to her personally to explain what happened nor any form of an apology.

Two months later Gabby met Tom face to face in the office of Madelyn Verdi, one of Freeport's other female attorneys. Gabby decided to engage someone from outside W&S to handle the divorce.

"Don't you have anything to say to me?" Gabby asked after they were seated in Verdi's conference room.

"I plead *nolo contendere.*"

"A *nolo* plea is not an admission of guilt, only that you have no defense. Was Judge Crockett in error?"

"No," came a whisper of a response, as Tom eyes refused to meet Gabby's.

"Anything you want to tell me about what I could have done to have prevented all of this?"

"Nothing to tell. It was all me and had nothing to do with you."

"Like hell, it had nothing to do with me!" Gabby slammed her hand down on the conference table so hard that water splashed out of the glass in front of her.

"What I mean is that there is nothing you could have done. It's all on me, and that's why I am not contesting anything. Whatever I have is yours. It's the least I can do under the circumstances."

Later Gabby realized that part of her anger during the meeting was indeed that of being denied her "pound of flesh."

Tom's insistence that he had no defense for his actions took away all of the righteous indignation she felt entitled to vent.

All he asked for were the few tools that had once belonged to his father. Gabby was left with her six year old Wrangler, all of the expensive tools, as well as the mortgage on Babcook Manor.

#   #   #

At some point during the night Gabby's half-conscious nightmare reliving of her divorce melts into a fitful sleep.

Chapter 19

The first Saturday outing to scout a vintage home designed by an earlier generation architect from Glenn's firm produces some interesting twists and turns, and not just on the back roads of Wisconsin.

Both sense, as they would later admit, a little tension. Gabby is hesitant to broach the subject of the mounting mystery of Babcook Manor even as it preys on her mind. Her periods of quiet come about when she ponders the potential consequences of letting Glenn in on her problems. She feels attracted to him and wants to confide, but she is hesitant. The fact that she is preoccupied becomes obvious at times, so Glenn begins to wonder if there is something wrong with him that is causing this beautiful, amazing woman to seem so distant.

Reasoning that she is having second thoughts about him because she knows so little about his past, Glenn decides to divert Gabby's attention on the long drive by talking about his life.

"You know that I grew up in what you up here call 'southern' Illinois. In reality, there is more of Illinois south of where I lived than north of it. But you northerners think anything south of I-80 is just a stone's throw from the Gulf of Mexico."

"You're probably right, but when almost seventy percent of the state's population lives above I-80, it's hard not to think of the rest of Illinois as 'down state.' Besides your downstaters think that anything north of I-80 borders on the Arctic Circle. And while we're on the subject, I hope that you were raised a Cub fan."

"Ahem, no. All of my family are die-hard Cardinal fans and have little tolerance for Cub fans."

"You poor child, to have been raised with such depraved indifference. We'll have to do something about that. The path to conversion is hard, but it can be accomplished if led by a truly dedicated teacher."

"Yeah, but that presents a conundrum as I may never be able to go home again if I convert. Besides, now that I live where there are Brewer fans, converting to the Cubs could be just as dangerous."

"Have faith, my Padawan, I will show you the path to Truth, Justice and the north side of Chicago."

"I thought you didn't go to movies."

"In general I don't, but I am not culturally illiterate. Besides, it was a favorite expression of my Ex, even though it is a mixed allusion, like most of his aphorisms."

"Uhhh, do you quote him often?"

"Not if I can help it." With that they both fall silent for several minutes as Glenn navigates his six year old Volvo along a Wisconsin county road. At length he decides that he needs to broach a part of his past that has yet to be discussed.

"At dinner last week we both mentioned that we're divorced. On my end, marriage was a case of mistaken identities. I was not what Alexi, my Ex, wanted me to be and she was not what I thought she was. We met while I was working as an intern finishing my master's degree in historic restoration. She was a landscape designer hired by the foundation that owned the house we were restoring.

"We began dating and after I landed the job in Madison we married. Ours was a massive, lavish wedding that was way beyond anything my family could ever have afforded. All of them felt out of place—the 'southern Illinois yokels' at a posh Chicago social affair. What I didn't pick up on during the time we were dating and engaged was that Alexi had dreams that were too big for Madison, or even Wisconsin. No sooner were we back from our honeymoon then she was on the hunt for a job with any company that was in the top ten of any category where they hired landscape designers.

"Eventually she was offered a job by the Architect of the Capitol. That's the office that does all of the work on the US Capitol in Washington. The job paid less than she was making, but she saw it as a means to enhance her resume and rub elbows with people who could advance her career. When I was hesitant about leaving Hunter, Jameson, she blew up. Told me there was no way she was going to spend her life as the wife of a so-so architect working for a so-so company in Wisconsin.

"Unless I could find a job in the DC area, there was no way we could afford to move there on the salary she was offered. I still had some college loans outstanding, let alone the cost of living there. She knew her parents would subsidize our living, but my pride wouldn't let me live off them. He dad is a successful real estate developer in the Chicago area. His Beemer cost more than I make a year, and he had no qualms about giving his 'little 'Lexi' everything she ever wanted.

"Faced with the ultimatum of either becoming what I saw as a 'hired husband' or staying put, I opted to remain in Madison. To make the rest of the story move along quicker than a glacier, I'll just say that we split up and she went to DC, filed for divorce, got a three story townhouse in Georgetown and is soon to be engaged to the son of a prominent Senator. Her new hubby will probably move into his father's Senate seat some day with an eye on the White House.

"On several occasions I have been tempted to contact him to warn him that if his career does not move quickly enough, he better look out, cause she'll be gone quicker than he can say 'filibuster.' I'm glad we never had any children, so at least no one else got hurt in the mess. Though I think for Alexi children will only be props for her climb to whatever she deems as the top."

"Sounds like we both were victims of hidden identities." With that comment, Gabby relates a brief summary of her failed marriage to Tom.

Chapter 20

Gabby and Glenn stop for lunch at a Culver's in a small Wisconsin town. They are about to finish their meal when an elderly couple sits down in a booth very close to their table. No sooner is the couple seated then the man begins haranguing his wife.

"You dumb bitch. I cannot believe you ordered soup. I never order soup unless it comes with the meal. Why would anyone ever pay for soup? You think I'm made of money? Just wait till we get home. You'll get yours, Miss Strumpet."

Throughout his condemnation, the woman sits with her head bowed and hands folded in her lap as if she is praying. Eventually the man grows quiet, but when their food is delivered he starts in again.

"Look at this shit. Why would anyone put the pickle on top of the bun? These dumb assed kids working in this place." As he speaks, he gets louder and louder so that eventually everyone in the place can hear him. "No wonder this country is going to hell in a hand basket. No respect or decency. Bunch of young punks think they can dump bullshit on old people. This is what comes from electing those liberals and socialists. No damn respect or sense of common ass decency."

"Maybe they put it there in case you don't want it, so it'll be easier to take off," the wife replies in a quiet voice.

"Who the hell asked you, smarty pants? You mind you own bees wax. When I get you home, there'll be hell to pay. I don't need some smart mouth witch telling me what's what. Damn you, I have half a mind…"

"Excuse me," Glenn interrupts as he stands at their booth. "Would you answer a question which all of us in here really want to know?

"Huuhh?"

"The burning question we are all asking ourselves is this: are you a real asshole, or do you just play one in real life?"

"What? What does that mean? Why, you can't talk to me like that!"

"I'll tell you what I can do. See this lady with me? She's an officer of the court. If we ever hear of you talking to this or any other woman like that again, or if we ever hear that you've harmed her in any way, we will have you arrested and thrown in jail. There's a very special jail for men like you who abuse women and you'll be sorry if you ever end up there. Now eat you food in silence and mind YOUR own business. Remember, we WILL be watching you."

With that Glenn turns and heads for the door, Gabby in close pursuit. She hears applause as they exit.

Once in the car, Gabby says, "Where did that come from?"

"Sorry," Glenn whispers as he seeks to catch his breath, his hand shaking as he tries to put the key in the ignition. "It just galls me when a guy bullies a woman. Something just snapped. I'm not even sure what I said to that old codger, but I know I was seeing red the whole time."

"What you said was pretty amazing and got a round of applause from the other patrons. Well done, Sir Galahad."

Chapter 21

When they arrive back at Babcook Manor there is again the awkwardness of whether their first kiss is to be the limit to the day's final scene. One kiss leads to another and another, but finally Glenn says he has to leave and when Gabby does not contradict him, he takes the hint and bids her adieu.

Gabby is about to get in the shower when she hears a noise from down in the garage. Taking her pistol from the gun safe hidden in the night stand next to her bed, she runs into Glenn at the door near the bottom of the stairs to her apartment.

"Geez Louise Gertrude! You don't have to pull a gun to get me to leave!"

"Sorry, I heard noises and lately I get pretty nervous around here at night."

"I got almost to the first traffic light when I remembered I brought you the original landscape plans for this place. I found them in another file at the office. Do you know how to use that big honkin' thing? What type of cannon is that?"

"I'm sorry. No, it's not a cannon. My grandfather brought it back from the war, and would often tell me, 'young lady, this is not just a gun it's a Colt 1911 Navy point four five caliber semi-automatic pistol.' I grew up using it at a shooting range. Dad gave it to me when I graduated law school and started living on my own. In case you haven't figured it out yet, Dad really wanted a son, but all he got was me. Hence guns, woodworking and being a diehard Cubs and Bears fan."

"Wow. Well, I'm very glad he didn't get a son. As for baseball, Alexi cured me of any desire to watch any sports. If there was no social climbing aspect to an activity, it was verboten. As to your fear of being alone, I would think that the new security system would have eased your mind about intruders. It's armed? The alarm system, I mean."

"The alarm in the house is armed any time I am not in there. I had yet to set the one here in the garage tonight. That's why when I heard noises I reacted the way I did."

"Is this area of town a hotbed of break-ins? Seems like a pretty good neighborhood."

"No. Not that I know of. I've only had one real problem since being here. Probably just some nosey kid, but it caused me to put in the alarm system. Besides, there are things about this place that keep me up at night, and they have nothing to do with nosey kids or what an alarm system can detect."

"Care to share or do we need to call Ghost Busters?"

"No, no haunting. At least not the type of ghosts you're thinking of. Well, I'm not going to easily fall asleep after this, so you might just as well come up and I'll fire up the Keurig. This will take a while to explain."

When Gabby finishes telling Glenn everything she knows or has been able to cobble together on the mysterious John Galway and Babcook Manor she shows him the Springfield sniper rifle and the strange diagram she found behind the mantle of the basement fireplace.

Examining the diagram Glenn comments, "This thin, see-through paper reminds me of that movie, a John Wayne flick I think." He snaps his fingers as he tries to recall the details of the film. "It was about World War II, and they were fighting the Japanese on some island. But they could not find where the enemy was hiding their artillery. Then they captured a Japanese soldier, I think, and he had a piece of paper like this. They finally figured out that it was a map overlay. When lined up correctly it showed where the enemy's artillery was located and which tunnels were used to move ammunition."

"You suppose that is what this is? That would explain the tracing paper. But where would you find the original map it was designed for? Be like looking for a misplaced comma in an unknown book somewhere in the Smithsonian."

Glenn looks at her with a funny expression on his face.

"Did I just say 'Smithsonian'? I've been hanging around Barnes too much."

"Barnes?"

"Doctor H. Elmer Barnes, the director of the local history museum. He helped me with some of the research on the house. He used to work in Washington."

Glenn sits there thinking, tapping his fingers on the rolled up landscape plans. Gabby brews more coffee as she too ponders where to begin looking for the map that would go with the diagram.

"If Galway hid this drawing in the house, he must have hidden the map, too," Glenn reasons.

"He never hinted about any other hiding spot. Although I have to admit that he has been dribbling out the clues in a most parsimonious manner. He still may have one that will lead to a map. And what if it's not a map overlay? Maybe it just refers to three spots which point to a fourth. Could be that the use of tracing paper was just a coincidence. Maybe even a red herring."

"You have those blueprints for the house here?"

"They're in the living room on the shelf above my desk." Gabby retrieves the plans and the two of them spend an hour moving the diagram around on each page trying to find three points that line up with the circles and make sense.

"Well, I give up. This could all be a wild goose chase. This drawing might not even be the same scale as the house plans."

"Agreed," sighs Gabby.

"I need to be getting back to Madison. At least I've had enough caffeine to keep me awake."

With that they re-enact the earlier goodnight kiss scene, though this time both are a little more passionate about it. The end result is the same and as Glenn leaves Gabby enters her code in the alarm system for the garage.

The shower water has no sooner begun to cascade down her body than an idea flashes like the spark from a nail hit by a hammer slightly off-center. Without taking even the time to soap up, she gets out of the shower, towels off, throws on some sweats and heads back to the kitchen.

Unrolling the single page landscape plan she begins sliding the diagram around on it. In no time at all she finds three trees whose locations fit the diagram. As she contemplates how accurate this might be, or whether or not it is just a coincidence that the drawing fits, she realizes that the plans are some eighty-five years old. The trees might not even still be there, and if they are, they will have grown to such an extent that what she assumes the numbers next to the lines on the tracing paper to indicate distances could therefore be off by several feet.

Without thinking of the time she grabs her cell phone and punches Glenn's number. When he answers she can hear the sounds of the wind from open car windows on the warm June night.

"What's up?"

"I think I found the key. The landscaping plans."

"Geez Louise Gertrude. I never thought of them and they were lying on the table all the time. Mom always said, 'there's no point in being stupid unless you show it once in a while.' So, what's next?"

"What time can you be here tomorrow: assuming you're up for an archeological dig?"

"Noon sound reasonable?"

"I'll be ready. Say, you got one of those laser devices that measures distances?"

"Got several at the office. Want me to bring one?"

"Might be helpful."

"Then it'll be closer to one before I get there by the time I swing by the office."

"OK. See you then. I'll have some lunch ready."

"Deal. Sleep tight."

"You, too."

Chapter 22

When Glenn arrives the next afternoon Gabby is just coming out of the garage with a shovel in hand. "Wasn't sure you'd show," she begins.

"Why?"

"That was some pretty heavy stuff I laid on you last night about all that's connected to this place. You sure you want to get involved?"

"If you're 'in,' then I'm 'in'."

With that Gabby gives him a quick kiss on the cheek followed by: "After Mass I went to Farm and Fleet for an extra shovel and big tarp to pile dirt on. I also identified the three trees that matched the ones on the landscape plan. The point of the intersecting lines is in the middle of open lawn."

Looking at the shovel Glenn queries, "You assuming we're going to have to dig?"

"I figure that the number next to the intersection of the lines is a depth. What else might it be?"

After a light lunch they use the laser to establish the distances, laying out each tangent with bright yellow string with wood stakes to hold the strings in place. Then they adjust the strings so that they meet at a point where all the distances marked on the diagram agree. Glenn marks a circle on the grass using a type of spray paint used by landscape contractors.

"The problem is, if the distances are for these trees when they were thirty or more years younger, we could be off by several feet," Glenn opines as he scratches his head.

"Well, then we'll have to keep widening the hole until we find it. Whatever 'it' is."

"This could take days using shovels. If we think the number is the depth, you're going to have a pretty big hole."

"Do you remember how to calculate the diameter of a circle?"

"I'm a licensed, professional architect, ma'am. Yes, I think I can calculate the diameter of a circle."

"Instead of starting out where we have the stake now, let's recalculate the distances shortening them to the size of the trees twenty-five years ago."

"But, we need to make some determination as to what their diameter was when the landscape plans were developed. It shows that the three trees were already on the property. These are big trees, maybe as much as a hundred years old. Without being able to see the growth rings to count the years, we have no baseline for any calculations."

"I see your point," grumps Gabby as she drops to the ground.

"How sure are you that the method we're using is correct?"

"I don't know. Maybe seventy-five per cent."

"You willing to put some money on that hunch?"

"Why?"

"Simplest solution would be to rent a backhoe to dig out the area. Since we have no idea how wide the hole will need to be, then the fastest, most efficient method would be to get a backhoe."

"What about a metal detector to help pinpoint the spot?"

"Do we know if what we're looking for is metal? And I'm not sure how deep they can detect. The drawing shows five feet, which may be way beyond the range of a typical metal detector."

"Well, shit and shoved in it!"

"Say what?"

"My Dad's favorite expression when he hits a snag. And we certainly keep running into them. OK, you win, where do we get a backhoe?"

"Have you ever run one? I haven't."

"No."

"Well, since neither of us has ever run one, and we'd need a truck to pull the trailer and the backhoe, it may be best to hire someone."

"I've got my pick-up."

"Yes, I noticed that monstrosity in the garage. Hemi, four-wheel drive, extended cab. Wow! Why did you purchase such a thing?"

"Is Mr. 'I-drive-a-Volvo-and-save-the-planet' passing judgment on my behemoth? She does have feelings you know."

"She? And yes, maybe a little judgmental here. Coupled with the Wrangler, you do seem to own vehicles that expand your carbon footprint."

"When Tom left, I got tired of hiring a truck to haul building materials. Then I mentioned over coffee one day in the office that I was thinking of buying a used pick-up, and one of the secretaries said her son needed to sell his. Poor kid. I felt so sorry for him when I went to buy it. It was his dream truck, all tricked out the way he wanted, but he had lost his job and he and his wife had a baby on the way, so he couldn't keep up the payments. The poor guy had tears in his eyes as I drove off in it."

"I see your point about feeling bad for the kid. And the Wrangler?"

"Gift from Dad after his midlife crisis dream car met the adamantine reality of Mom struggling to get in and out of it. So it's a hand-me-down because my very old Civic was on its last legs."

"Well, does the pick-up have a trailer hitch and the necessary electrical set-up for trailer lights and breaks?"

"No."

"Then we're back to hiring someone."

"What do we tell the guy about why we want the hole?"

"We can think of something."

"Yeah, what? Come dig a big hole in my backyard for the fun of it?"

"Wait, the original landscape plans called for a pond," Glenn says as he unrolls them. "It was located about where we've marked. That may be why Galway buried it so deep. He was filling in the old pond and put whatever 'it' is at the deepest point. So, we'll just say we want to recreate that pond. Six feet deep around the area where we think this 'thing' is buried."

"Why six feet. The diagram says five."

"Top soil around here can add up to a tenth of an inch per year, so if this thing was buried as long as forty years ago, we better go deeper than the five feet."

"Agreed. Let's go lay out the dimensions of the original pond using stakes and spray paint. I'll find a contractor tomorrow and see when he can be here."

Chapter 23

The plan works; at just over five feet down, and within two feet of the original spot they plotted, the backhoe pulls up an object about two feet long by a foot in diameter. It is wrapped in Visqueen.

Trying to be nonchalant about the find, Glenn retrieves it after the backhoe operator points it out. Glenn gives it to Gabby who lays it against the side of the garage.

Soon Glenn tells the contractor to stop. "The lady has decided this is going to be too big and is making too big of a mess."

"Women! Well, you've already run up the minimum charge, so if you want me to quit, I will. You want me the fill it back in?"

"No, she may change her mind again. If not, she can fill it in herself since this was her bright idea."

"Women, don't ya just love 'em?"

Glenn feels bad about letting the contractor think it is just Gabby being a stereo-typical woman who couldn't make up her mind, but it seems the easiest way to terminate the dig without arousing suspicion.

The mystery bundle sits next to the garage until the contractor loads his equipment and leaves. Using the knife that Glenn always carries in a sheath on his belt, Gabby carefully cuts through the layers of Visqueen as Glenn's fingers gently hold open the incisions like a surgeon's retractor. They are amazed that the interior is dry. What they find, however, does not cause much enthusiasm: a pair of blue jeans, a grey chambray shirt, a worn and stained ball cap with the insignia missing, a tan windbreaker, and a pair of expensive, very thin but well-tailored leather gloves.

Nothing about the bundle is remarkable until Gabby finds a folded piece of paper in a pocket of the windbreaker.

"This appears to be a torn off piece of newspaper. One side has 'Chicago *Tribune*, November 10, 1963' printed on it.

89

The other side has a series of handwritten numbers and letters: '66S 69S 75S.' Mean anything to you?"

Both stare at each other in silence. Just finding something where the diagram pointed has Glenn finally believing fully in Gabby's story about Galway, even as Gabby is frustrated at finding yet another puzzle piece which does not seem to connect to any of the others.

Chapter 24

The next Saturday, which turns into a hot, sultry, corn-growing Midwestern kind of day, Gabby and Glenn work with shovels and wheel barrows filling in hole. The past week was rainless, so the dirt is dry and easy to handle. They first spend almost an hour digging in the bottom of the hole, "just to be sure," but find nothing else.

Glenn works fast, loading, moving and dumping two loads to Gabby's one. But within an hour he is ready to collapse.

"You gotta learn to pace yourself," Gabby smiles as she keeps going.

After fifteen minutes under shade, Glenn is back at it, but he paces himself with Gabby.

The hole is completely filled by the time the sun begins to slide behind the tall trees on the west edge of Babcook Manor's lawn. Bringing bottles of cold water from the garage, Gabby hands one to Glenn as they both drop exhausted to the grass in the shade of the huge oak. A tree that is one of the three they used to locate the hole.

"I have to admit," Glenn begins as he looks at Gabby, "this was a labor intensive way to do it but being out in the sun today sure brought out your freckles."

"What's that supposed to mean? Just because you were abused as a child, being raised as a Cardinals fan doesn't mean you can heap abuse on others."

Unsure whether or not Gabby is kidding, Glenn stammers, "Only meant that I like them. They are really cute."

"Cute is it? Do you know how much crap I had to take from kids when I was in grade school over these? I was so upset once that my mother caught me sitting on the kitchen floor at two in the morning trying to rub them off using Comet cleanser. So, I am proud of them and don't take kindly to having fun made of them."

"Gabby, I was not making fun…"

"Gee, Glenn, get a grip, I was just yanking your chain." With that she leans over and kisses him.

After a brief period during which they stare into each other's eyes, Glenn clears his throat and asks, "Well, got any other buttons I can push that will get the same response?"

"You'll have to figure that out for yourself."

They lay back on the grass, fingers entwined as they stare at the moving glimpses of light filtering through oak leaves.

"Glenn, I've got to ask at this juncture, are you sure you want to get involved in this whole Galway thing? It's my problem because I own the house, but as Dad would say, 'You don't have a dog in the fight'."

"No offense meant, but I do have a dog in this fight— you. If you're in, then I'm game for wherever it leads us."

"What did you mean, 'no offense meant'?"

"I did not mean to imply that you are a dog by any stretch. I was just following your analogy."

"Oh, I see." With that she leans over and kisses him again. "Thanks for agreeing to stick with me."

"My pleasure, but if we have to get out the Ouija Board to figure this out, I'm not going down that road."

"Deal. And I hope it doesn't come to that."

After a few minutes silence as each wanders off into their own thoughts, Glenn says, "I guess we can safely state that this was not the 'glory hole' we had hoped."

"I hate the thought of going back to see Galway without having more ammunition. The information you get out of him is Delphic in its ambiguity."

"What if we tackled him together? He's never met me."

"You mean both of us go see him?"

"Sure, maybe it'll get him to open up a little more."

Chapter 25

The next morning, after Sunday Mass, Gabby meets Glenn at Higher Grounds, his trip home to Madison that evening and then back to Freeport having been uneventful. After rehashing the evidence and finishing their lattes they drive over to The Haven to see Galway. At first he is suspicious of Glenn, but eventually he just ignores him.

Revealing the fact that they have found the clothes buried in the backyard does not solicit much of a response and Galway is not forthcoming regarding any of the questions Gabby asks.

When Gabby pushes him, Galway begins to curse and reaches for the call light switch. His cursing at Gabby brings Glenn out of his seat and as he steps toward Galway, Gabby puts her hand on Glenn's arm saying, "Easy, Sir Galahad."

Galway instinctively feels why Glenn has moved, so the cursing stops. Gabby says they are leaving, but then Galway asks, "Do you know what Guiteau and Czolgosz had in common?"

"Who?"

"Guiteau and Czolgosz."

"What am I supposed to figure out now?"

Galway falls silent and then pretends to doze off, ignoring Gabby's question.

The drive back from The Haven begins in silence but Gabby is suddenly hit by an idea and makes a quick right turn off Galena Avenue onto West Street. It is Sunday and they have not called ahead, but she hopes that Barnes will not take offense at their dropping in unannounced.

They find him wearing a wide brimmed straw hat, khaki slacks and an Oxford cloth shirt as he pulls weeds from the flower bed along the east side of his home. Much to Gabby's relief, Barnes is delighted to see them, finding their visit an excuse to stop working in the hot sun and oppressive humidity. He is also pleased to meet Glenn, even more so when Glenn says that he is a specialist in historic restorations.

"Come, we'll sit on the veranda and I'll get some iced tea. I've my own recipe you know." In a way that Gabby always finds delightful, Barnes waves an index finger in the air as he heads for his back door. The veranda is screened in and well shaded. Ceiling fans make the place feel almost air conditioned.

After tall glasses of tea are handed around, Barnes begins, "Well, what new facts do we seek today?"

"What did Guiteau and Zoo-log-sky have in common?" Gabby queries.

"Who?"

"Zolgossy, we think," Glenn tries to clarify.

"Do you mean Czolgosz?"

"Yes, that's it, I think."

"Oh, well if it's Leon Czolgosz, he assassinated President McKinley in 1901."

"What did he have in common with Guiteau?"

"Oh, besides the fact that they both killed Presidents, both were insane and both were executed for their crimes. I am not aware of anything else. Some twenty years elapsed between the two assassinations."

"I think we're looking for something that connected them to Freeport, maybe."

"Hmmm. That's a tough one. What brought this question to mind?"

Gabby and Glenn look at each other. They are both thinking about whether or not to bring Barnes in on their mystery. Finally, Gabby decides that it will make things easier if he knows, so they fill him in on all that they know and how they obtained the information.

When they finish, Barnes comments, "That's a remarkable tale. I would suggest that the clues Galway has been giving you have been lucid enough that I do not think he is suffering from dementia. They seem well thought out. Now back to Charlie and Leon. Hmmm. I seem to recall that one thing they had in common was that after they were arrested both asked to speak to Jane Addams. That would be a tenuous

Stephenson County connection for the two. I'm afraid that I'd have to do some research to go beyond that tidbit."

"Would there be any information that might provide answers in the Museum's archives on the Guiteau?" Gabby speculates.

"I'm afraid that avenue of research will prove fruitless. The Guiteau family was so humiliated by the deed of Charles that they made a determined effort to leave little of themselves for posterity. More iced tea, anyone?"

The three sit and chat for almost another hour before Gabby and Glenn get up to leave. As they are walking to their car, Barnes fills them in on the family of Jane Addams and her father's relationship with Abraham Lincoln.

"Lincoln actually addressed John Addams as 'My Dear Double-D Addams.' Of course, he was accustomed to names with double Ds because of his wife's maiden name."

Chapter 26

G abby, however, has yet another twist of the story handed to her on Monday, when a letter arrives at her office. It has no return address and the cancellation is some suburban Chicago mail processing center. Inside, is a single piece of paper with three typewritten lines: two lines of numbers—one with fifteen digits, and the other with eleven— and a third line, with the words "Credit Suisse."

Checking the Internet, Gabby discovers that Credit Suisse is one of the two largest banks in Switzerland. Going to the bank's website she clicks on the account access icon, finds the place to enter account numbers and then keys in the fifteen digit number. Where it asks for a PIN, she uses the eleven digit number.

Within seconds the screen shows an account holding 2,781,212 Euros. The currency calculator translates that into 3,689,320 in US dollars.

Gabby sits slumped back in her chair staring at her screen when Sam comes bouncing into her office.

"Gabby, you look like you've seen a ghost. You Okay?"

"Uhhh. Yeah, I think so."

Just as Gabby is about to click out of the account, the screen asks if she wants to transfer or withdraw funds. Realizing that she has access to all that money, she swallows hard but then hits "escape."

"You sure you're OK?"

"Yes, Sam. I'm fine. What do you have there?"

"Well, the National Personnel Records Center in Saint Louis finally sent us the service records of Sean Michael Fallon. Probably took longer because we did not have his service number. Anyway it seems that Fallon entered the Army in 1943 at age eighteen. He was quickly noted as an expert marksman and given advanced training. His time in Europe, roughly from August 1944 to January 1945 was spent as a sniper. His file notes that he voluntarily transferred to the Office of Strategic Services on 1 February 1945."

"I'm surprised that access to such records isn't restricted to immediate family," Gabby speculates.

"The rules state that they are, except that sixty-two years after leaving the military the records are open to other people. In this case, since the records center thinks that Fallon is deceased, they were not in the least hesitant about sending a copy."

"Dead?"

"That's what is indicated on this cover sheet. Says they were informed in 1964 that he had died. One of those grave markers for veterans was authorized but no one ever requested it. This thing is sorta one of those enigma things inside one of those like riddles."

"You got that right."

Chapter 27

That night, not waiting for Glenn's return the next weekend, Gabby puts on her leather tool belt and begins rooting around Babcook Manor trying to find anything that might be the hiding place alluded to in Galway's last clue.

Ever since the alarm system was installed Gabby has been leaving on the exterior lights 24/7. Rather than have them go on and off with the timer at sunrise / sunset she decided that if they are on all the time so that anyone watching the house will never know if someone is there or not. She also leaves the lights inside the house on all the time figuring that it will be easy to see from her garage apartment if anyone is moving around inside the house.

Since she is poking around inside the house that night, the alarm system is not armed as one of its functions is detecting motion within the house. After almost an hour of finding nothing intriguing, she sits down on floor in the hallway of the second floor to think. That's when she hears a noise from downstairs. Quietly she pulls the .45 out of her leather tool bag and slides across the hardwood floor to the top of the stairs.

The sound of breaking glass tells her someone is trying to get the kitchen door open. Doing her best imitation of a ninja warrior, she moves silently down the stairs, her heart pounding in her ears as she holds the pistol upright in both hands. The sound of the kitchen door swinging open is followed by footsteps crushing broken glass.

Gabby reaches the bottom of the stairs and takes a quick peek around the corner to see what is down the hall in the direction of the kitchen. She sees a shadow moving on the wall opposite the kitchen archway, so she pulls back. Thinking she can slip across the hall and through the open door into the dining room, she starts off the bottom step only to come face to face with a man wearing a hoodie. He is at the far end of the hall and freezes when he sees her, just as her movements stop when she sees him. He is backlit by the light in the kitchen such that Gabby cannot make out his facial features.

The tableau of mutual shock quickly dissolves when his eyes spots the gun in her hands. In a split second he is moving toward the back door of the kitchen, glass crunching under his feet. Animated by his movement, Gabby runs after him. When she reaches the patio, she stops as she watches his dark figure sprinting across the lawn toward the back fence. Partially due to the adrenaline and partially due to irritation over the break-in attempt, she takes careful aim, firing one round into the trunk of the large oak tree closest to where she stands.

Bet that scared the shit out of you crosses Gabby's mind as the intruder disappears into the darkness.

Turning to look at the door, she can see that he has used something to break the glass next to the doorknob. Without looking back at the track taken by the would-be robber, she goes across to the garage, punches in her code to disarm its alarm and then retrieves a broom and dustpan.

Gabby has just finished sweeping up the glass when a Freeport police car, emergency lights flashing, pulls up to the garage. The sight of the police shocks her into realizing that Babcook Manor is not an island unto itself. There are neighbors in close proximity. The first officer is exiting his car when a second car arrives.

"Ma'am, we've reports of gun fire from this residence. Are you the owner?"

"Yes, officer. Someone tried to break in. You can see the door's broken glass," she answers while holding out the dustpan full of glass.

"Who fired the shots?"

"Shot. Only one round, officer."

"Did you fire it?"

"Yes."

"I need you to put your gun down on the ground." This command is spoken as both officers put hands on weapons.

"Ma'am, please hand over your weapon and move very slowly."

"Officer, I do not have the pistol on me."

"Now! I need to see that weapon now!"

Gabby holds out her hands, one holding the dustpan and the other the broom and then turns around slowly. "Do you see a gun on me?"

"It's against the law to discharge a firearm inside the city of Freeport, so I need that weapon handed over now, or tell us where to find it."

"This property is NOT in the city of Freeport. You have no jurisdiction here. You can take my gun, you can even arrest me, but I promise you that tomorrow the States Attorney will kick the case only after he kicks your sorry butts out of his office."

"That may be, but we must have the gun. We can get a search warrant if need be."

"I think Murphy's Law just became operative in this situation. Okay, have it your way. It's in my tool bag in the garage. If you want to accompany me inside to get it, you may do so." With that Gabby lays down the broom and dust pan.

"You're giving us permission to enter the premises?" one of the officers asks.

"Yes."

The other officer accompanies Gabby into the garage.

"It's in that bag on the workbench and is no longer loaded. The clip is next to the gun."

Slowly Gabby opens the bag then steps back from the workbench.

After putting on a pair of vinyl gloves, the officer places the gun and its clip into an evidence bag, seals it and writes on the outside.

Having secured the gun in his squad car, the officer comes back with a clipboard and sits down next to Gabby, who is now seated on the patio. Asking a series of questions about the incident, he takes notes. At one point she has to go to the apartment above the garage to retrieve her driver's license and Illinois Firearm Owners ID. When she hands them to the officer, she also gives him her business card.

"You're an attorney?"

"Yes."

"You do know it is against city ordinances to discharge a gun inside the city?"

"Yes, I am fully aware of that, but this property is not inside the city. But we'll sort that out with the State's Attorney if you are going to arrest me."

"Given your position in the community, we will not detain you at this time. However, if the investigation proves otherwise, we will be back."

"Understood, but your time might be better spent looking for the guy who broke the glass on that door."

"You do know you could have hurt someone simply by firing into the air, even if you weren't aiming at someone?"

"Officer, I am fully aware of such dangers. If you examine that tree, at a height of about five feet off the ground, you should find the spot my slug impacted. I am a very good shot and I always hit what I aim for."

The other officer, realizing the futility of continuing the verbal skirmish over the gun, intervenes at this point to ask about the would-be intruder. Gabby describes the man and points in the direction of his flight.

Chapter 28

The next day, not long after Gabby arranges for Freeport Glass to replace the broken pane on the kitchen door, a retired city police officer stops by her office.

"Miss Gordon, I am Alden Lapp. The Chief of Police called me to ask if I would share some history of Babcook Manor with you," begins the very elderly, but distinguished black man who speaks softly but with a dignity that commands attention.

"Do you have some past connection with the place?"

"Well, since I am now the oldest retired city police officer still alive and I was part of one incident at the manor, I suspect that the Chief thought we should chat."

"Please, have a seat, Mr. Lapp. Can I get you a cup of coffee? Water? Soft drink?"

"No, thank you, ma'am. I won't take but a few minutes of your time. I was just a rookie on the city police force when we got a call of an incident at Babcook Manor. I was partnered with Corporal Larry Frueh; he was my training officer. Anyway, we went out to the manor as it was reported that someone had shot a dog that belonged to a Mr. Flaherty. A German shepherd it was. Beautiful animal. Someone had hit it with an arrow that went through the poor dog's body and stuck out both sides. Reminded me of those comic hats with the pretend arrow through the head, but this time it was not so funny.

"The dog was still alive and we radioed for the station to find a veterinarian to come see if the dog could be saved. After almost an hour of calling, it seemed that not one veterinarian in the area would touch the dog. Now we were workin' with two men who seemed to be guards on the property. So they called Mr. Flaherty in Chicago and he sent his helicopter to get the dog.

"I'd never seen a helicopter before and to think that one person could own one was amazing. Anyway, before the helicopter arrived the police chief was on the scene. He took over talking to the two guards. Once the helicopter left, we went back on patrol. The next day, when we reported for duty, the chief had a meeting of all the officers on the force. We were instructed to never respond to a call at Babcook Manor unless the chief himself told us it was okay."

"Was that because the house is not in the city limits?"

"No, it was to insure that we did not stumble into something that might best be left unknown, if you follow my meaning."

"Did they find out who shot the dog?"

"The chief somehow figured it out. According to what Frueh told me later, the chief told the guy that if he valued his life, he needed to leave town that day and never come back. I never heard any more about it. But the chief's order stood. No one answered a call to go to the Manor without the chief's okay. Although I have to say that in all the years I was on the force, I never heard of another call to the place."

"That is an amazing story. Mr. Flaherty must have had some deep pockets to send a helicopter from Chicago all the way out here just to pick-up a wounded dog."

"Yes, ma'am. Also, the chief wanted me to tell you about the only other incident on record for Babcook Manor. That was eight years ago when nine-one-one received a report of a drunk woman walking along River Road. A squad car arrived just as the woman's husband got there. According to the report, of which I have a copy here for you, it was a Mary Alice Galway and a John Galway. They were residents of Babcook Manor and both suffered from Alzheimer's disease; she was not drunk. They were transported to Freeport Memorial Hospital and eventually became residents of The Haven nursing home."

"I always heard that the house had been abandoned for forty years," Gabby says as she seeks to get more information on who knew Galway was living there.

"We knew somebody was living there, but for the most part no one ever saw whoever it was. Never any other complaints or reason for us to approach the place in all those years. And, as you are already aware, it is not within the jurisdiction of the city. Well, I won't take any more of your time. It was nice to meet you."

With that Lapp stands, removes a large envelope from his brief case and lays it on Gabby's desk.

Without taking time to look inside, Gabby extends her hand saying, "Mr. Lapp, it has been my honor to have met you. Thank you for taking the time to come see me. Let me walk you to the door."

"That's not necessary. Have a nice day."

Just as Gabby is about to sit back down at her desk, Lapp sticks his head back in her office door and adds "I almost forgot to tell you. They saved that dog. A year later it was back on the grounds running around like nothing happened. All the vets here were afraid to touch it because of the rumors about Flaherty. But someone did a good job fixin' that poor dog. Good day, now."

Lifting the envelope Gabby can tell from the weight that it's her grandfather's .45.

Chapter 29

The Historical Museum's Annual Ice Cream Social is an event that Gabby has been remiss in attending since leaving the Museum's Board. This year she decides to go, mostly out a sense of obligation to Barnes for his help with Babcook Manor's history, but with Glenn making so many trips to Freeport lately she decides not to ask him to accompany her. As she now sits at a table alone, she begins to question that decision—not that she is self-conscious about being alone in social situations, but the recent events with the attempted break-in and Galway's machinations have her somewhat off balance.

She is about to bolt down her ice cream and head for her car when she sees Barnes heading her way with two elderly ladies in tow.

"Gabriel, so good to see you here. I have some ladies you ought to meet. This is LaVerne and Maxene St. Andrews. Ladies, I'd like you to meet Gabriel Gordon."

"Nice to meet you, but you don't have to ask, we'll just tell you up front," begins Maxene. "Yes, we have a sister named Patty, but she doesn't live here anymore."

"Our parents thought they were being so clever naming their three daughters after the Andrews Sisters…"

"Actually, Patty and I were born before the Andrews sisters became a big act, but Mama wanted to complete the set when our youngest sister was born, so LaVerne it was," interrupts Maxene, pointing to her sister.

"As I was saying, Mama and Papa liked the idea especially given our last name, but it has not been easy on us," adds LaVerne with a touch of annoyance as she shakes her head.

Gabby starts to tell them that she isn't sure who the Andrews Sisters are and she certainly has no idea what their names are, but LaVerne jumps in before Gabby can get a word out.

"We don't sing and we don't own any of their records."

"That having been said" interrupts Barnes, "Maxene here used to work at Babcook Manor in the early 1950s, so I thought you two ought to have a chat."

"Yes, I am a registered nurse and I used to visit Babcook Manor three times a week while PWJ and Ethel were alive. PWJ is what we called P.W. Babcook, Jr."

"Maxene was the major medical provider for PWJ for over five years. We understand from Harry that you now own Babcook Manor."

"Harry?"

"I'm sorry my dear," Barnes interjects with as much disdain in his voice as he can muster. "That is what the 'H' stands for. Obviously, I prefer NOT to use it, but SOME people insist on dragging it into every conversation they've ever had about me. Now, if you'll excuse me I'll go someplace where I won't have to be subjected to abuse." With that he walks off, his ubiquitous cane swinging with a deliberation that mirrors his obvious state of agitation.

"Isn't he just the cutest thing? Maxene and I would just love to take him home and cuddle him forever."

"Somehow I never thought of Dr. Barnes as cuddly. Certainly dapper and debonair, but not particularly cuddly," observes Gabby.

"My sister tends to exaggerate only a tad. Please forgive her."

"Don't be sarcastic dear sister."

"Why, LaVerne, I don't even know how to spell 'sarcastic,' so how can I be that way?"

"Oh, sister, I only say what I think. He is so…"

"LaVerne!" with that LaVerne falls silent. Maxene continues, "Now, Miss Gordon, you wanted to hear about my experiences at Babcook Manor?"

"That would be interesting. Please sit down. Have you had your ice cream and pie?"

"Oh, heavens yes. But LaVerne is planning on going back for seconds, weren't you, dear?"

"Sister, are you trying to get rid of me?"

106

"No, just wanting to talk with Miss Gordon without being interrupted every time I pause to take a breath. Now run along dear and have some more ice cream and maybe they'll have some of Linda's wonderful raspberry pie left."

Once LaVerne is out of earshot, Maxene sits down and begins a monologue on her time at Babcook Manor.

"I was just out of the St. Francis School of Nursing when I was hired by the Babcook family to help with the care of PWJ. He was in his thirties by that time and rapidly approaching the age when most people with Downs died back then. You did know that he had Down Syndrome? Back then people with that condition were referred to as Mongoloid. The barbarity of it all! Today, the average life expectancy for Downs patients is into their 60s.

"Old man Babcook had seen to it that his son lived in isolation and confinement. Such a pity as we now know that many Downs patients can develop mentally, though at a slower rate than the rest of the population.

"When P.W. died he left poor Ethel to care for his son. Ethel was equipped neither emotionally nor physically to deal with her step-brother. Consequently she allowed him to roam the grounds of Babcook Manor during the day, almost like a wild man. Many were the times when I would arrive and no one could find him. In the middle of winter he might be outside for hours wearing no coat, no hat and sometimes no shoes.

"More's the pity, but when the poor man died, he was found out in the woods behind the house, sitting against the base of a tree, havin' taken off all his clothes. And that was in late November, mind you.

"Well, Ethel may have been relieved to have him gone from her care, but she quickly fell into deep depression. Guilt for how she'd treated her half-brother if you ask me. I continued my visits, monitoring Ethel's medical condition— she suffered from curvature of the spine and had great difficulty getting around. Confined to a wheel chair the last two years of her life, you know.

"All my experiences with the Babcook family, one of the richest in this town's history, showed me that God may hand out riches to some people but that is no guarantee they will be any happier than the rest of us. Indeed, in the case of the Babcooks there was a great deal of unhappiness."

"They are out of raspberry pie, sister. And did you tell her about that poor child being chained in the basement?" asks LaVerne as she returns, shoveling ice cream in her mouth.

"No, sister. I am sure Miss Gordon has no desire to hear the gruesome details of that poor man's troubled existence."

"So they chained PWJ in the basement?"

"I did not know that when I was seeing him as his nurse. Emily told me after he passed. I suppose it was her way of trying to confess her sins. But PW had a secret room built under the stairs in the basement and they would put that poor man in there at night, chained to the wall, so he wouldn't go running around town. Apparently Old Man Babcook thought it was degrading to his family name to have the citizens of Freeport calling the police when they saw PWJ roaming the streets in the middle of the night wearing nothing but his all togethers."

"Tell her about eatin' raw squirrels," adds LaVerne through another mouthful of ice cream.

"You'll have to excuse my sister. Her's has been a sheltered life for the most part. She has always lived at home. In the last twenty years she has been taking care of me. Before that she took care of Mother and Father after she lost her job at the telephone company."

"Fifty-one years ago," LaVerne resumes as she waves her spoon at Gabby. "When they switched from operator calls to direct dial, it put one hundred-sixty of us out of work in one day. Only job I ever had. After that I stayed home. Patty ran off to marry, of all things, a man who worked for the telephone company. And after the way I was treated by the phone company. She was such a traitor to the family."

"We like to say that Patty fell in love with long distance, which is not original, but it pretty much sums up what happened."

"And we never saw her again. She ended up in some God-forsaken place in the mountains of Pennsylvania. Now they live in Florida on his fat pension, a pension I would have today if they hadn't automated. And now we're stuck here dealing with these horrid winters. You'd think they'd at least invite us to come visit."

"Oh, Dr. Barnes, glad you're back," Gabby sighs.

"Come, my dear, I've someone else I want you to meet. Thank you ladies for filling Miss Gordon in on Babcook Manor."

As they walk away, Gabby whispers to Barnes, "Thank you for rescuing me."

"I know my dear. The only way to get rid of them is to thimblerig some excuse to pawn them off on someone else. But then I begin to feel guilty, so I always end up coming back if I see the conversation has become a marathon."

"So, who did you want me to meet?"

"Oh, heavens, no one. It was just a ruse to get you released from the talons of the St. Andrews sisters. Paradoxically, one always wants to wear the Cross of St. Andrew on one's lapel to these events in the hope of warding off those two witches. To quote Shakespeare, whenever I see them at a distance I think to myself, 'by the pricking of my thumbs, something wicked this way comes.' "

"Why Doctor Barnes, I have never heard you speak ill of another person."

"If you had to endure those two as I have for years, you would consider my comments mild indeed. Both of them have delusions of marrying me. Can you imagine such a catastrophe? The two are supposed to be worth considerable sums of money and I have been warned by several people to keep in their good graces lest they drop the museum from their wills. I suspect that they intentionally irritate me, as well as the director of the art museum, knowing that we are obliged to suck it up. In truth, they'll probably die and we'll discover that their fortune is rather small and they were misanthropes who have left what little fortune there is to some obscure home for wayward orphan witches."

With that Gabby and Barnes bid goodbye as she heads home.

Chapter 30

Once back in her apartment Gabby falls into a speculative mood, her feelings of missing Glenn at the ice cream social causing her to further examine their relationship.

Both divorced, they seem to share a tendency to shy away from rushing into a deeper relationship. Perhaps both sense that in each other they see something worth taking things slow and easy. If either had been interested in a quick fling, then this sense of letting things develop on its own timetable would not be so apparent.

Gabby recalls when Glenn went grocery shopping with her a week ago. He knew how to check the eggs in the carton to make sure none were broken. *The boy's had some basic training. He's a keeper* she thought at the time as she smiled inwardly.

And the whole episode at the Culvers with the abusive husband. Got to like a guy who is intolerant of those who abuse others.

He is caring without smothering, thoughtful without being solicitous. Brought flowers once, but did not make a habit of it. Gabby appreciates romantic gestures, but would have been wary of a guy who sent flowers one day and expected the relationship to jump to new levels the next.

In truth, Gabby is enjoying just the simple thrill of romance. She dated very little in high school. Being a qualifier for the state finals in debate three years straight, as well as carrying a 4.0 GPA and being intolerant to the clownish antics of most boys her own age, meant that guys generally avoided asking her out. Just so she could go to prom her senior year she felt compelled to ask a debater from another school.

In college, the absence of the debate scholarship meant that she had to work all of her free time. Her only socializing in college had been with the other girls with whom she shared a four bed room apartment. Fortunately, all of them were inclined against random sex, so there was never a problem with any of her roommates having overnight "guests" and then an awkward moment the next morning at the bathroom door with some unexpected male.

The relationship with her Ex had arisen out of their mutual interest in carpentry, but it later became clear that Tom's interests could not stay focused. Gabby had heard other divorced women talk about their "practice marriages," but still does not think of her marriage to Tom in that context. While not making light of a failed marriage, she somehow feels that their relationship was a speed bump that showed her that to be successful a relationship had to be built on a meaningful foundation. She concluded that saw dust and sex alone could not be mixed into a mortar that could long hold together a marriage.

In her relationship with Glenn, when she is truly honest with herself, she acknowledges that she really likes knowing that someone cares for her and thinks about her and wants to be with her—an emotion she never felt with Tom. Not that she has an inferiority complex, but she has never thought of her inner self as being someone sought out by other people. Professionally, socially and intellectually she makes satisfying connections with other adults, but emotionally this is the first time she feels a real connection with another human. And it all feels incredibly liberating.

Chapter 31

L ater that night Gabby goes into Babcook Manor to look for the hidden room that is supposed to have been PWJ's nightly prison. It is so well hidden that when she painted the walls of the basement she had not noticed the camouflaged door in the bead board enclosing the space under the stairs. Poking and prodding, she finally finds the spot that needs to be pushed to release the spring hinged door. Inside is a set of shackles anchored to the cement wall.

Standing there, staring in horror at the chains, Gabby jumps in fright when her cell phone rings. It's Glenn. She tells him all about her conversation with the St. Andrews sisters and how she found the secret room under the stairs.

"It's called a 'spandrel,'" Glenn comments.

"The chains?"

"No, the space under a staircase is called a 'spandrel.' You'll have to keep up with these architectural terms as we go along."

"That's architect-speak for a prison or just a place to catch dust?"

"Well, the space can be used for many things, though I doubt that the original architect envisioned this spandrel being used as a detention cell."

After the brief conversation, she stands looking into the spandrel when something catches her eye. The pattern of dust on the floor is not the product of fifty years of dust settling randomly out of the air. It is in a pattern that sweeps from left to right, appearing as if someone scattered the dust with a sweeping hand motion, a right-hand motion. *That's odd, very odd.*

Eschewing the thick layer of dust and the cobwebs, she crawls inside to examine the space. The deliberate pattern of dust suggests that someone wanted to disguise the fact that they had been inside. After several minutes of poking around, all the time avoiding touching the shackles, she concludes that nothing is hidden there. Crawling back out, she brushes the dust off her pants and cobwebs off her cap.

In her thoughts, Gabby's gaze remains fixed on the shackles even after she closes the door. Yet another image that she does not want in her head.

Chapter 32

The day after the Ice Cream Social is a Friday, and Gabby is plowing through a stack of documents related to a will she is preparing for probate. Her train of thought is broken when Sam taps on her door. There is a glower on her face.

"Joe Blunt here to see you."

Shit and shoved in it! runs through Gabby's mind.

Joe Blunt is a real estate agent whose advertising slogan is "If a house you hunt, call Joe Blunt." At 5' 7" and sporting a belly bulge that bespeaks too many hours drinking coffee and eating pie at the various rumor mills in town, he is an agent who seems to relish taking on properties that are the hardest to move. It was through Joe that Gabby and Tom purchased Babcook Manor.

As he comes into her office and offers a handshake, as is his custom, Gabby hesitates, but then takes his hand.

"Good to see you, Gabby. Just stopped by to see if you're ready to put Babcook Manor back on the market. We're reaching midway through 2010 and the real estate market is beginning to pick up, and this would be a great time to get out there. The house and property look great and I am sure we can get you a good deal. Just let me know when you're ready."

With that, he is gone, leaving Gabby standing there with her mouth slightly agape. Her blank thoughts are broken when Sam takes her right hand and pumps hand sanitizer in it. It is commonly known around town that Joe Blunt never washes his hands after trips to the bathroom.

"Like, when are you going to start keeping your office door closed? It is hard for me to brush off creeps like Blunt when they can actually see you sitting at your desk. The other attorneys keep their doors closed."

"I know. It just makes me feel cooped up."

With that Sam is gone and Gabby sits back down to the task at hand.

Two hours later she has yet to reach the bottom of the pile of documents when Sam again sticks her head in the door. This time there is a broad grin on her face as if she'd just learned a hot piece of gossip.

"There's a gentleman here to see you. Says he's an architect, and doesn't have an appointment. If you've got no use for him, he can like study my blueprints anytime he wants."

Smiling as she stands and turns toward the door, Gabby says in jest, "Sam, stop that."

"As my mom would say, 'He's built like a brick shithouse on a paved alley'."

Walking out to the waiting area Gabby is pleased to see Glenn's smiling face.

"Came to see if Freeport's next Clarence Darrow is free for lunch."

"Somehow you don't become a Darrow while executing wills and planning estates. But, yes, I am free for lunch." When Gabby tells Sam that she is going out for lunch, Sam winks and whispers, "Where've you been like hiding him?"

"I'm not telling."

As they head for the door, Glenn asks, "What's with your secretary? She just keeps grinning at me."

"Don't worry, she doesn't get out much," Gabby replies just loud enough for Sam to hear. Sam sticks out her tongue at Gabby in retort.

At Gabby's suggestion they walk over to 9 East Coffee. After a scrumptious soup and salad they stroll over to Debate Square where Gabby gives an impromptu lecture on the debate between Abraham Lincoln and Stephen A. Douglas that was held there in 1858.

As they walk around Glenn reads the signage about the history of the debate. He stops when he comes to the sign which tells about President Theodore Roosevelt coming to Freeport in 1903 to dedicate a monument to the debate. Like the other signs in the Square this one reproduces a front page from a local newspaper which carried original reporting on the event described on the sign.

"Hey, did you ever notice this? This is the front page from *The Daily Democrat* of June third, nineteen oh three. All of the page deals with Roosevelt's visit here, but in the upper right hand column is a story about an assassination attempt that was foiled."

"You've got to be kidding. I never knew that," Gabby says as she begins reading over Glenn's shoulder. "Wait a minute! I do know about that. Galway's uncle was the guy who found the bomb. He was a grandy dancer...no, that's not it... a gandy dancer, a guy who worked maintaining the tracks. He worked for the Chicago and Alton Railroad, as did Galway's father. Amazing."

"Yeah. The things you can learn reading signs at historic sites. Like the History Channel but without axes and alligators."

The warm June afternoon inspires them to sit on one of the shaded benches. While sitting there Gabby tells Glenn about the intruder, the brush with the local gendarmerie, and then the information on Babcook gleaned from the St. Andrews sisters.

"Why didn't you call me after the break in?"

"What could you have done at that point? It was after ten PM when the police finally left, and I did not want you to drive down here and then have to go to work the next day. The glass in the door has been replaced and things are back to normal."

"Not my point. I worry about you being there alone with all these unanswered questions. I'd feel better if I knew you were willing to call me any time, not just when you think it won't inconvenience me. Can I count on you for that?"

"Yes, I promise to let you know when anything else happens. But don't be annoyed that Dad raised his only child to be self-reliant and independent."

"And maybe a little bit stubborn, too? Anyway, perhaps you shouldn't be living there alone."

"Volunteering to move in?"

"Well, I…I…just…I…" stammers Glenn.

"Oh, don't take this too seriously. I wasn't asking for a commitment or anything. Relax." Gabby laughs at Glenn's red face and seeming discomfort. Glenn does not see much humor in it.

"Sorry. I guess you caught me off guard with a subject I have been thinking about recently."

"Tired of the drives late at night?"

"Not as tired of the drives as I am of having to say goodbye to you all the time."

Good answer she thinks.

"Well, with the alarm system I'm not worried," Gabby adds.

"Packin' that .45 adds a little extra insurance, too."

"I would not want to rely too heavily on it. I was just lucky to have had it in my tool bag that night. Don't know what made me take it along. Anyway, I think I managed to scare the crap out of the jerk."

They sit for a time just enjoying the quiet together. Finally, Gabby says she has work to do and needs to head back to the office.

As they walk past Freeport Public Library, Glenn comments on its architecture, "That is an impressive design. Does the interior follow the exterior's neo art deco theme?"

"Why don't you explore it this afternoon? I'll be home around five and we'll whip up some supper before we begin thinking about how to make some sense out of Galway's clues."

"Let me take care of supper."

"OK. Here's the key to the garage. The code for the alarm is your license plate number backwards."

"Really?"

"Yes, but I'll be changing it tomorrow." Then she begins to grin at the look of disappointment on Glenn's face.

"You're so mean."

Glenn leaves Gabby at the street level entrance to the office building where her law firm is located. When she gets to her office there is a single red rose lying on her desk. Sticking her head out the door of her office, she asks Sam, "Where'd this come from?"

"No idea, but if I had it like checked for finger prints, they'd actually belong to a hunk of an architect that someone's been hiding."

Gabby smiles and shrugs. Plopping back down at her desk she sniffs the rose as she swivels back and forth in her chair.

Chapter 33

Glenn cooks up an excellent seafood linguine that evening, so they linger over dinner and a bottle of wine longer than they had planned. As they clean up the dishes Glenn notes, "You know it would be fun to cook in that gourmet kitchen you put in the big house."

"You're complaining about the limitations of this kitchen?"

"Well it does leave something to be desired. Not enough room if one person sautés while another person tries to uncork a bottle of wine."

"Whine, wine. That's your problem. Let's go walk around and see if something strikes us as related to the crazy clue about Guiteau and Czolgosz."

"You know, it occurred to me that we have taken this all wrong. Czolgosz's name has two 'Zs' and Guiteau's name has two 'Us'. Maybe that's the clue—double letters."

"Give it up, Sam Spade. Galway isn't that clever."

At Glenn's suggestion they begin sorting through the boxes and dilapidated furniture that belonged to Galway and are now stored in the third bay of the garage. Using Glenn's knife Gabby cuts open the cushions of the sofa and two stuffed chairs that comprise the total of the "living room" furniture. Then she attacks the fabric that is stapled to the bottoms of each item. Nothing.

"I give up" she says after wrestling the bulky pieces around. "This last clue is so opaque even Sherlock Holmes would ask Sir Arthur for a new occupation."

Glenn sorts through the boxes of what turn out to be mostly books. "Well, at least we know what they did with their time all those years. There are hundreds of paperbacks here. Mostly westerns—Louis L'Amour and Zane Grey. Beyond that, I don't see anything that might help."

As he continues to dig, finally he exclaims, "Well, here's a history of Stephenson County from 1970! This could explain where he got the information he has been using to give hints based on local history."

With that, Glenn plops down on the couch and begins looking through the history. Gabby is just returning with bottles of water when he calls, "Here it is. Page 70. And I quote, 'Lincoln's letters to him were to 'My Dear Double-D Addams.' That's what Barnes said. Maybe that's the meaning of the Jane Addams connection to Guiteau and Czolgosz."

"Would you give up on the double letter thing?"

A further fifteen minutes spent reading aloud all passages in the history book regarding Jane Addams and Charles Guiteau prove fruitless. Lacking any better idea they decide to revert to their original plan to walk the grounds rehashing the clues, evidence and theories that have accumulated in their conscious minds like the gossamer wings of milkweed seeds in a spider's web.

Eventually, they find themselves walking along the wrought iron fence that runs like a demarcation line along River Road. Glenn stops at about the mid-point, leans back against the fence and gazes up at the house. Gabby steps away from the fence, walks a few feet toward the house, and then turns back to Glenn. "Guiteau, Czolgosz, Garfield, McKinley, Addams. I think Galway is flat-out whacko and is just playing us."

Staring wide eyed at the house, Glenn burst out, "Wait! What was it that Lincoln wrote to Addams?"

"Ahh. Something about 'My dear Double-D Addams.' Are you back on that again?"

"Can you say staring us in the face? I knew it had to do with double letters, oh ye of little faith. Look at the front of the house."

Gabby turns to look at Babcook Manor, but nothing catches her eye. "And see what?"

"Double 'D!' "

"Where?"

"That huge bronze letter "B" on the turret."

"What? No! Oh, shit and shoved in it. Can that be it?"

"It must have been made in two parts because it's so big. Block letters that look like two 'Ds" one atop the other to make a 'B'. The bottom one is slightly larger than the one on top."

"No! No! No! This bastard is playing mind games and we're his patsies. You're just seeing things, like in ink blots, or in clouds that look like whales, just filling in the missing spaces to make sense of it based on his suggestions."

They half walk and half trot up to the front of the house under the "Double D," and begin looking for possible hiding places. None of the masonry of the turret seems to have been removed or re-tuck-pointed.

"You supposed he buried something in the ground under here?"

"Only one way to find out. You get a couple flashlights and I'll grab the shovels."

Ten minutes later, after Glenn removes a layer of dirt to the depth of the about a foot, his shovel clangs when it hits a metal object. Like greedy prospectors who at last have seen some glimmer of gold, the two drop to their knees and begin digging with their hands. In minutes they have an eight by six by four inch metal box pulled from the hole. The hinged lid is locked, so they take it into the garage not wanting to bang on it with a shovel for fear of ruining the contents.

Using a bent paperclip Glenn fiddles with the lock mechanism, which turns out to be a simple design. Without too much effort he gets the lock to move and the latch pops up. They look at each other before opening the lid. *Are we again going to find disappointment at the end of another thrilling hunt?*

Slowly Gabby raises the lid. As light spreads into the recess of the box, it is reflected off a jumbled pile of metal. Reaching into the pile, Glenn brings out a bunch of shell casings strung onto a chain with a set of military dog tags. Closer examination shows that the tags were issued by the U.S. Army to Sean M. Fallon.

The shell casings have holes drilled in them to allow for placement on the chain. Glenn looks at each casing and says to

121

Gabby, "I can make-out the outline of letters and numbers on these."

Using some brass polish Gabby retrieves from a cabinet, they clean off the tarnish on each casing which they later determined are .30-06—the size used in the Springfield Model 1903A4 sniper rifle Gabby found in the garage attic. Engraved on each casing is a location followed by a date.

"These are souvenirs of Galway's kills," Glenn whispers. "There are twenty-seven of them."

"Look at the dates," Gabby adds. "They begin in 1944 and run up to 1961."

"This guy was one sick bastard, keeping the shell casing from each of his hits and then having them engraved with the dates and locations. I'll bet if we took these to him right now he could tell us the names of each victim."

Gabby throws the collection back into the box and slams the lid shut. "That's just too disgusting to contemplate. Why would someone do this? Why would he want us to find it?"

"Just like I said," Glenn answers. "Trophies. He's bragging. Wants someone to know how many lives he took."

If Gabby has had trouble sleeping through the night before the double "D" discovery, it is nothing to how she feels after finding Galway's chain of mementos.

Chapter 34

Half an hour later they are seated at the tiny table in the apartment's kitchen, both swirling wine in their glasses as they swirl all they know about the situation in their minds. Finally, Gabby stands up, walks to the counter and picks up a knife.

"Let's summarize what we know. But let's do it out loud so we can hear each other say it. Maybe that'll help make more sense of it. I don't have one of those white boards, so we'll just do it orally."

"You need a knife to do that?"

"No, just wanted something to keep my hands busy." She lays down the knife and leans back against the counter. As if presenting a closing argument for a jury, Gabby begins.

"So, we have a man who was a highly decorated sniper in the US Army in World War II who ends up working for the OSS, precursor of the CIA. Stands to reason that the OSS and probably the CIA used his marksmanship on problems they wanted solved.

"He marries the only daughter of a man heavily involved in organized crime in Chicago. Sometime in the early 1960s he goes to ground here, living under an assumed name, in a house owned by his father-in-law's family. For forty years he and his wife live here, virtual prisoners. The last ten years they never leave the property and for the last two years they never even leave the house."

"But then she gets Alzheimer's and he can't take care of her in their hideout," continues Glenn. "So he has to have her committed to a nursing home, but he fakes dementia so he can be near her. Real love."

"Or, he's afraid that she'll start talking. The janitor at The Haven said that when Mary Alice was alive Galway would not leave her alone with anyone else."

After a pause Glenn starts again, "And what's up with those walls around the tennis court and the swimming pool?

I'm not an engineer, but I know enough to know that they were not designed to ever support a roof."

"Assuming that the walls did not pre-date Galway's time here, maybe he wanted privacy."

"I could see some reason to maybe swim in the nude, but play tennis *au naturale* is a bit too much."

"It would give new meaning to 'forty love'," Gabby says dryly.

The conversation pauses and again it is Glenn who resumes thinking out loud.

"She dies and then he discovers that you've bought this house and you're going to resell it. So he contacts you and begins giving hints about mysterious stuff hidden on the grounds and in the buildings. Stuff he undoubtedly put here."

"Wait, he didn't know I was going to flip the house when he contacted me. He just thought that I had bought it to live in."

"So why put you on the trail of his hidden past?"

"Did he know that there was that weird slip of newsprint in the jacket with the numbers and letters on it? And what do they mean?"

"Where does Mrs. Hannigan come into this? She's got a bone to pick with the Celtic law firm, so she tips you off about Galway's real name and the Swiss bank account that belongs to him and his deceased wife."

"The rifle has a scope, which could mean that it was used by a sniper."

"But why hide any of this stuff? He could have walked across the road to the river and thrown all of it in there and no one would ever know about any of it."

"Perhaps he held on to the gun thinking that someday he might have to come out of retirement. When Mary Alice suddenly lost contact with reality he was caught short and did not have time to dump the stuff."

"Unless he wanted to have some evidence in case something went wrong. To prove he did or did not do something."

"The logical conclusion is that he shot someone, someone really important, and he lived the rest of his life fearing that he'd be caught."

"Then why keep the evidence? If he's accused, the existence of the rifle could be used as evidence."

"What if it wasn't the police he was afraid of? If he whacked some mafia bigwig, then he would have to fear the gang of the guy he whacked more than the cops."

"That might explain the walls around the tennis court. He was afraid that a sniper like himself would take him out while he was practicing his back hand."

"But then we're still back to why keep the rifle?"

"Self-protection?"

"It would have taken a good hour to get to the gun. And we have never found any ammunition for it. Although we keep finding stuff hidden around here, so maybe we've just not found any yet. But if it's that well hidden, he'd have to see them coming days away for the rifle to have been of use."

"Maybe he thought his own gang buddies would give him a heads up if someone was coming for him."

"I would bet that none of his buddies knew where he was. Far as they knew, he had dropped off the face of the earth."

"Or was dead. He said his sister in Florida thinks he's dead, and we know that the military records center thinks that."

"So, what have we left out of this speculation marathon?" asks Glenn.

"The Swiss bank account. That's one hell of a lot of money. Nobody gets that big of a pay-off unless it was for whacking someone of major import."

With that they both fall into silence. While there is no sound in the room, their brains were whirring in high gear as they try to make the pieces of the puzzle fit into something that makes sense.

Chapter 35

The unmistakable sound of shattering glass literally cuts into their thinking. In a split second Gabby is at the window looking at the back door of the manor. "Someone is opening the door."

"You set the alarm?"

"Yeah. The alarm company should call within minutes to see if it's a false alarm. They'll call the sheriff if I don't answer or if I answer and tell them it's not a false alarm."

"So we just sit and wait for the cavalry to arrive?"

"No way. Who knows how long that will take?" Gabby is into her bedroom in seconds and returns with her .45.

"Surely you're not going down there to confront this...this... hoodlum?"

"If he knows where something is hidden in the house that would make sense of all of this, then I don't want to risk him getting away before the sheriff gets here. Besides, I would prefer to question him myself." With that Gabby pulls out her cell phone to call the alarm company to tell them it's a false alarm.

"You really want to confront this jerk? He might be some drug-crazed bad ass just looking to grab enough stuff to fence for a new score. And now you've called off the cavalry."

"I think you've been watching too much TV with all that jargon. We can go out the back of the garage so that the noise of the overhead doors doesn't spook him. We'll wait in the shadows behind the garage for him to come out. That way we'll be between him and his prior escape route."

When they are outside, peering around the back of the garage toward the open kitchen door, Glenn whispers, "I'll go over there in the shadow of that tree. If he tries to get past you, then he'll head that way and I can cut him off."

"With what? If he's got a gun..."

"If he's got a gun, then you'll have to say so out loud when you confront him so I'll know. If he doesn't know I'm there, then I can jump him from behind as he passes."

The sounds of crickets fill the warm night as Glenn moves toward the tree's shadow, staying beyond the outer edge of the pool of illumination thrown down by the patio lights.

After almost twenty minutes the figure emerges from the house and looks up at the apartment windows. He appears to weigh his options. As he starts for the back fence Gabby steps out from behind the garage, levels her gun and says softly, "Stop."

The man starts to reach for something in the small of his back, but he freezes when he sees Gabby's .45 pointed at him.

"Don't try to reach for that gun. Why have you come back?"

"Never been chere 'fore, lady. How 'bout puttin' da artillery way?"

"Not a chance. You were here about a week ago."

"Not me. Never been chere 'fore, lady."

"What you looking for in the house?"

"Tryin' to score somethin' to fence."

"Not buying that. You're too clean to be a junkie."

"Look, lady. Just calm down and I be outta chere in a flash."

"No way. Cops are on the way. We'll just wait. And keep your hands where I can see them."

At the mention of the cops, the man becomes very nervous. He looks around, almost like he's going to reveal a secret. Then he leans toward Gabby in a conspiratorial manner. "Look, lady. I'm juz lookin' for a 'torney name Scurry. Owes my boss a boat load o' money but he's gone on da lam. Word on da street is dat he was headed chere 'cause he had money stashed in dis house."

"How did you get that info?"

"My boss, Jimmy da Flea, he a bookie and dis Scurry prick's into him for over a hundred Gs. Then Scurry doubles down on da Notre Dame-Navy game. Figures it's a cinch with da point spread. But da Irish choked and now Scurry he owe Jimmy over three hundred Gs, and Jimmy mean to collect."

"But how'd you find out that Scurry was headed here and had money here?"

"One of da other 'tornies in Scurry's office also owe Jimmy over that same Notre Dame game, so he traded da info for a reduced sentence, so to speak."

"How'd this source know that there was money hidden in the house?"

"Say Scurry told him some old codger had been saltin' way cash for forty years."

"You ever heard of John Galway or Sean Fallon?"

"Nope. Can't say I has. Look, lady. I juz casin' da house lookin' for Scurry. Jimmy, he wanna cap Scurry in da knees, not get da money. Wanna make a zample outta him cuz he's such a high roller in da city."

"What's your name?"

"Look, lady, I gotta get outta here if dem cops is comin'. I told ya da 411 on this Scurry guy, so's you can be ready when you see him."

"How am I supposed to know who he is? Maybe you're really Scurry."

"I figured you knew him seein' as you never asked his full name."

"Your name?"

"I gotta scoot, lady."

"Name?"

"Schicchi. Gianni Schicchi."

"OK, Gianni, scram. If you know what's good, you'll stay away from here. The house is alarmed. Even if I hadn't been here, the cops would have shown up any way."

With that Gianni strolls off into the darkness of the backyard, his hands over his head. They heard him utter a few swear words when he momentarily gets caught on the fence.

Chapter 36

L ater that night Glenn reluctantly goes back to Madison since he has a company outing the next day—Saturday. After a sleepless night Gabby goes to her office in the morning to use the Internet. She wants to see if she can track down Hannigan.

Finding a letter to Tom from Sean M. Scurry in the file concerning the purchase of Babcook Manor, Gabby notes the initials "SMS:mhh" on the bottom, indicating who had prepared the letter for Scurry's signature. Putting M. Hannigan in a search engine for Chicago telephone numbers, she gets four hits. One of them, a Mary Hannigan has a middle name of Helen—"mhh."

Using the office phone Gabby dials the number listed for Mary Helen Hannigan. A man answers.

"I am calling for Helen Hannigan. This is Gabriel Gordon."

"This is Alex James. When was the last time you talked to Helen Hannigan?"

"Why, it's been several weeks. It was at the law offices where she works. Is there something wrong? Who is this?"

"This is the Chicago Police Department. Helen Hannigan and her daughter Fiona have been reported missing. Neither has shown up for work in the past week. Their employers called us. We are now going through the Hannigans' apartment looking for any information on where they might be. What is your business with her?"

"Her law firm handled one end of a real estate sale and Mrs. Hannigan said that I could contact her if I had any questions. I know it seems odd that I would be calling her at home on a Saturday, but I was hoping she could recall some facts."

"Well, I see from the caller ID on this phone that you are calling from Weston and Sanderson in Freeport, Illinois. Your name is Gordon?

"Yes, Gabriel. I am an attorney with Weston and Sanderson."

"If we have more questions we'll want to get in touch with you. It would help if you gave me your cell phone number." After the detective writes down Gabby's number, he continues, "If you happen to hear from the Hannigans, please call the Chicago PD. My name Alex James, Detective James."

After Gabby gets off the phone she begins to have a bad feeling deep in the pit of her stomach. Retrieving the letter with the Swiss bank account numbers from her office safe, Gabby goes on-line to Credit Suisse. To her shock, the account shows a balance of about 150,000 in U.S. dollars, meaning that 3.5 million has been withdrawn in just the past few days.

Clicking on various pull-downs she finally finds one that allows her to examine the account's history. It shows that the account was getting interest added quarterly and that every six months the equivalent of $150,000 was being withdrawn through a transfer to an unspecified bank. However, the same day that Gabby had first checked the account the over 2.6 million Euros was transferred out sometime after she logged off.

Chapter 37

Gabby decides to have another confrontation with Galway. Heading from her office down Galena, she senses that she's being followed. If "Gianni" is following her, it is hard to tell, but there is that feeling. She even back tracks on a couple streets to see if she can catch sight of any car trying to duplicate her turns. No luck.

She finds Galway sitting in his usual position, back to the door, facing a window looking out into the fenced in courtyard. She has become a regular enough visitor that she no longer warrants an escort to his room. There is no change of expression on his face when he catches sight of her.

"Well, Mr. Fallon, you have been leading me a merry chase. I hope you are ready to come clean on all this or will this be our last meeting?"

"Unless you've figured out the house, I've got nothin' to tell you."

"What, no more riddles? How about I give you one? What do you call a guy whose Swiss bank account had three point five million dollars taken out in the last week?"

"You shittin' me?"

"No sir. On Wednesday there was somewhere around four point six million in there and today there's only around a hundred fifty grand."

"That little bitch! I've a good mind to go to Florida myself and take off her pimply head with a ball bat."

"Talking about your sister? Somehow I don't think it was her."

"What makes you say that?"

"Did you ever give her your account number and pass code?"

"I've never seen the account number and pass code. The lawyers are supposed to take care of the finances. You said there was only four point six million in there?"

"Yes, I checked on Wednesday."

"Should have been somethin' over five million."

"Well, someone has been taking out around a hundred fifty thousand every six months for several years."

"It's those blood suckin' lawyers. They think I'm on my death bed and they're lootin' my account." He sits and thinks for several minutes before he continues, "How did you get access to that account? You workin' for those crooks in Chicago?"

"No. Someone sent the codes to me in an anonymous letter. I think it was a secretary at that law firm. She must have realized that one of her employers was ripping off your account and wanted you to know."

"Mary Helen Hannigan?"

"Yes, that's who I believe sent the letter. It was unsigned. You know her?" Gabby asks in an effort to see what more Galway will tell her.

"Her husband was a cousin. He passed away about five years ago. He brought Mary Alice and me cash twice a year. For a long time he was the only human being we talked to year in and year out, except for Jack. Sometimes Mary Helen came with him. Mary Alice always liked that."

"Well, now Mary Helen and her daughter have gone missing. The Chicago police are looking into her disappearance."

"Probably the bastard who is siphonin' off my money figured out that she knew and had her eliminated."

"That's a pretty serious charge."

"Missy, you have no idea the kinds of people you're dealin' with. They'd kill ya for a hundred bucks, let alone a million."

"I have no illusions about the types of people involved in your business. We found your bundle of clothes. Still in pretty good shape. How long were they buried?"

"Close to fifty years, but who says I buried 'em? Find anythin' else of interest?"

"No. The rifle and the clothes. So unless you've got more information to divulge, I suppose we no longer have any business." Gabby has decided to keep the finding of the dog tag

132

/ shell casing set to herself for the time being, if for no other reasons than she does not want to listen to Galway gloat.

"Actually, we do. Now that I know that those blood suckers in Chicago have been rippin' me off, I want to retain you as my lawyer. What kind of retainer do you want?"

"Depends on what you want me to do for you."

"I'll want you to take over paying my expenses here to start with and then medical bills, though those are few now that Mary Alice is gone."

"We can get you on Social Security and Medicare."

"If I ever had a Social Security number I forgot it. Besides, I never had a regular job once I left the ..."

"CIA?"

"Yeah. Plus I don't want anyone findin' me."

"Is there anything else you'll need done that an attorney can perform?"

"I want to draw up a Will."

"I'll bring along a stenographer the next time I visit. She'll record..."

"No! All of this is between you and me. No one else." This is said with such force that Gabby senses that any further discussion would be pointless.

"OK. I'll draw up a contract for a retainer and then we can set to work on your Will."

As Gabby starts out the door of his room, he holds out an envelope with her name on it.

"What's this?"

He does not answer.

Chapter 38

As is her custom after Sunday Mass and every other morning of the week, Gabby goes to Higher Grounds. She has just logged on to the Internet when she looks up to see Glenn's smiling face moving toward her. She jumps up, gives him a tight hug saying, "I didn't expect to see you until this afternoon."

"I wanted to tell you about something I learned yesterday, so I came down early."

"Must be really important if you got out of bed before breakfast."

"Don't be critical. Can I get you anything?" he says as he heads for the counter.

"I'm good, thanks."

Gabby is getting ready to enter a search using the "66S 69S 75S" sequence when Glenn returns. As he sits back down, he asks, "Do you know the name of the girl working at the cash register?"

"Uhh, no…wait. I think its Karen. No, more exotic Kieran. That's it Kieran Shaw. Nice Irish name. Been here only about a week. Why?"

"She seems incredibly nice and pretty. Wasn't wearing a name tag, so I was just curious.

Before Gabby can hit "enter," for the Google search Glenn begins, "Anyway, about yesterday. We held my company's strategic planning session yesterday at the home of Tony Baylor, a senior partner who also happens to be a gun collector. I asked him about the rifle you found. Turns out he has one in his collection. By the way it's commonly known as a 'thirty-ought-six.' Anyway, Tony showed his to me. While I was looking at his I noticed that it did not have threading on the end of the barrel, like Galway's. When I asked why a gun would have such threading, he said it was probably for a sound suppressor—a silencer."

"Hmmm. I would think that if you're a sniper wanting to whack someone and get away, many be a silencer would be an asset."

"Tony said that a silencer for that rifle would be pretty big and heavy. It would have made the rifle harder to hold steady. And, he's willing to buy yours if you are interested in selling."

"At this point we probably ought to hang on to it. Who knows where all of this will lead…?" Gabby stops in mid-sentence as she sees a woman approaching their table.

"Gabby Gordon, it has been a long time," gushes the woman who is wearing more jingling jewelry than a shaman.

Gabby rises, extending her hand as she says, "Abbey, it has been a long time. Five years ago?"

"Yes. I am so-o-o glad I ran into you. The Women's Guild is soliciting for more members, ya know. It's free to join, but we are really trying to build like an actual network to like then develop some fun events to raise dollars for scholarships. If we can get your Email address, we would really like to include you in our network." Abbey is very animated when she speaks, using her hands and head to emphasize points in her conversation.

Fishing in her wallet Gabby produces her business card and hands it to Abbey. "It's on my card."

"Oh, that's just fantastic! We look forward to having you part of the team."

"Excuse me Abbey this is Glenn Logan, an architect from Madison. Glenn, this is Abbey…uhh…"

"Cogar. Cogar-Finney. Hyphenated last name. Wanted to keep my maiden name. Professional reasons." With that she put her hands on her hips and smiles broadly.

"What profession are you in?" asks Glenn, repressing a grin.

"I own a previously-used clothing store, 'Time After Time.' "

"I hope business is doing well."

"Fantastic! This economy has made quality used clothing a really thriving business. Well, I've gotta run. We'll be in touch, Gabby. It was such fun running into you and your friend. Have a good day."

After she is out the door Glenn looks at Gabby and says under his breath, "High school cheerleader." Gabby burst out laughing so loudly that everyone in the place stops talking to look at her.

Self-consciously, she leans in toward Glenn to whisper, "I was just thinking the same thing."

"And what's up with those finger nails all trimmed off with square ends?" Glenn puzzles.

"They're called French nails. A new old fad."

"Well, I guess I am just out of it when it comes to the latest of anything."

Reaching into her purse, Gabby hands Glenn the envelope that Galway gave her the day before.

"Who's this from?"

"Galway."

The note, handwritten by Galway, reads, *JWB drilled a hole in the door.*

"Who the heck is JWB and what does drilling holes in doors mean?" Glenn queries after reading the note three times.

"We must surmise that Galway has produced yet another arcane clue."

Turning from the note, Gabby updates Glenn on the latest from her meeting with Galway and on Mary Helen Hannigan's disappearance.

"Gabby, I'm worried about you. You can't go around playing fast draw with these folks. One of these times you're going to run into somebody too stupid not to try to shoot you."

"I suppose you're right. So, where are we with all of this?"

"At minimum, the silencer for the rifle is still to be found. And now we've got this JWB clue to deal with? No other hint from Galway?"

"No. He was too worked up about the missing money."

"It'll be interesting what you find out when you put together his Will."

136

"We'll have to be careful with all that. Once we ink a retainer agreement, anything he tells me will be covered by client-attorney privilege. I'll not be able to share it with you."

"Never thought of that. There'll be barbed wire on both sides of that fence. Get more info but you'll be unable to tell me any of it."

There is a group consisting of four couples sitting at tables at the far end of the coffee shop. They are having an animated discussion about local politics that is getting louder by the minute. Glenn nods toward the group and shakes his head.

"They're here every Sunday. All go to Mass at St. Thomas and then gather here. I call them the Roncalli Club," Gabby comments as she follows Glenn's gaze.

"The what?"

"Roncalli Club, for Angelo Giuseppe Roncalli, who became Pope John the Twenty-third. He was the pope in the 1960s who opened the doors of the Church to a broader view of the world and our role in it."

"Well, it's quite a lively group."

"They have some pretty interesting discussions. I'd say they are more liberal than the average Catholic around these parts, hence my nickname for them."

Looking at Glenn as he watches the Roncalli Club, Gabby realizes just how much she has come to care for him. Impulsively she says, "I've decided that double letter thing you figured out was a pretty good piece of detective work. From now on you'll be my 'Double N' guy."

Taken off guard by the comment, Glenn stammers for a moment trying to find the right words. Finally, he hits upon the correct response, at least as far as Gabby is concerned, "If it's from you, then its fine with me."

As another group of people comes in the door, Glenn suggests that they carry on their discussion about Galway in a more private place. They finish their breakfasts and then head to Babcook Manor.

Chapter 39

After getting glasses of iced tea they sit on the patio hoping to enjoy the open air before the day's heat becomes too oppressive. Gabby fills Glenn in on her discovery of the large transfer of funds from Galway's Swiss bank account. Quickly the conversation turns to a discussion of where to go next with their mystery investigation. Gabby has just stretched back in her chair when her cell chirps. She gives Glenn a raised eyebrow when she sees the caller ID.

The phone conversation is pretty much one sided as her responses are limited to "yes" "no" and "I see." When she terminates the call, she looks at Glenn saying, "Well, that's interesting. It was the Chicago police detective I talked to yesterday. Seems they've traced Mary Helen Hannigan and her daughter Fiona on a flight from O'Hare to Los Angeles and then on to New Zealand. From there they flew to Apia, Samoa."

"Where is Samoa and why go there?"

"Somewhere in the South Pacific, but get this, it has no extradition treaty with the US."

"Geeze Louise Gertrude!" Glenn whistles. "Do you suppose Hannigan was the one ripping off the Galway account?"

"Could be, but if that is the case, why would she have put me on to it? I would suggest that she knew that with my snooping around sooner or later the axe would fall on whoever at her law firm was stealing from the account and she might have some culpability, even if she just suspected but had done nothing to report it."

"This thing just gets more weirder by the minute."

"Really, 'more weirder?'"

"Sorry, sometimes I fall back into my stoner days."

"You? A stoner? Not likely, Double N."

"I know, but I like to pretend I have a more colorful past than a milk-white associate architect at a medium-sized Midwestern firm."

138

"Anyway, we still have more questions than answers. Certainly the Hannigans fleeing US jurisdiction will cause the police to look into the Irish law firm. Maybe that was also part of her motive: get the cops to shine a light inside the darkness of Malloy and company."

"So, where do we go from here?"

"Let's go to my office and use the Internet to do a little snooping. I was going to launch a query on the numbers/letters we found in the jacket when you showed up."

"Sorry. I have always been bad at timing."

"No, it was a good thing. Probably shouldn't run that search on a public Wi-Fi."

Chapter 40

Wh
hen they get to the office, Gabby first pulls up the Credit Suisse account. It shows a balance of only $20.

"Well, somebody hit the account again. Only twenty bucks left in it now. Last transaction was yesterday at fifteen thirty-six Greenwich Mean Time. Wonder what the minimum balance is for a numbered Swiss bank account these days? Do service fees kick-in at some point?"

"You suppose that was the Hannigans?"

"No way to tell at this point. If the police get on to the case, they may get the Swiss to disclose where the funds were transferred. I don't know anything about Swiss banking laws, so your guess is as good as mine at this point."

"Should you tell the police about the account?"

"I will have no authority until Galway officially hires me. Then it will be his call. If the police are in any way competent in their investigation, they'll check all of the accounts to which Hannigan had access. If they don't trip over this one, then we're in the wrong business."

"What if Hannigan had no access to the account?"

"It would seem strange that she would know the details of the account without having authorization to access it. Scurry is such a chauvinist he probably had Hannigan make the transfers for him—too lazy to even do his own stealing. Of course, she might have guessed that someone was stealing from it. But who sent me the account number and the PIN if it wasn't Hannigan? I doubt Scurry would and I seriously doubt that the jerk knows how to use a real typewriter."

Gabby turns back to her monitor and clicks on her Email. One message catches her eye. The subject: "Galway." Clicking on it, she notes that it came from a source that ends with "WS." That is a TLD with which she is not familiar. Later she will learn that the Email originated from Samoa. There is no way to trace it further.

"Oh, my. This must be from Hannigan. It reads: 'Watch your back. The original thief will think you took it, and he's prone to violence. We just got some of the crumbs. Poor Galway will be left with nothing.'"

"Sounds like she probably took the three plus million."

"They probably figured they were owed it for what Fiona was put through by that sleaze ball Scurry. Do you think that Scurry could have been the insider who was bilking the Galway account? It would explain how Hannigan knew, as she was his secretary. It would also explain why he got so testy when I pressed him on who was paying the bills for Galway. The history of the bank account showed that someone was withdrawing about a hundred fifty thousand every six months for a number of years back. Galway's medical and nursing home bills would not exceed three hundred thousand a year, would they?"

"It would be a pretty expensive nursing home to have expenses that high, especially in Freeport. Didn't Galway tell you that there should have been over five million? Even assuming that his numbers are based on the balance from eight years ago, that's a big chunk for nursing home expenses, I would think."

"We better look into nursing home insurance if that's the case."

"Well, let's tackle those mysterious numbers and letters."

Gabby keys into Google the sequence: 66S 69S 75S. The results are mostly PGA scores with a smattering of other sports scores and one link for Hereford cattle ratings.

"Well, that's a bust. Any other ideas?"

"Not really. Let's go find some lunch and chew on it for a while."

"Very punny."

141

Chapter 41

Back at Babcook, they linger over a salad lunch as Gabby savors the scrumptious salad dressing Glenn whipped up. Their conversation keeps coming back to the note referencing JWB.

"Maybe we're looking at this from the wrong side. All of the clues, except for the ones that led me to the rifle and the clothes, were about presidential assassins. Was there one with the initials JWB?"

"Of course," Glenn exclaims. "John Wilkes Booth. He killed Lincoln. Why didn't I think of that sooner?"

"So, did Booth drill a hole in a door?"

"Yeah. He drilled a small hole in the door of the theatre box where Lincoln was supposed to sit that night. That way he could see inside before he opened the door."

"Then we need to look for a door with a hole drilled in it. I don't recall seeing any in the house when I was remodeling. I would remember that because I'd have had to fill the hole, sand it down, and then refinish. I didn't have to refinish any of the doors."

"I figured you re-did the front door. It looks like new."

"It is new. The old one was in really bad shape. Galway had screwed steel brackets to the back and the door jambs so he could place a couple two by sixes across it, and …oh, yeah! There was one of those peep holes at eye level so you could see who was on the front porch without opening the door."

"I suppose the door went to the dump or some such."

"No," Gabby says with mounting excitement. "Dad and I lugged the heavy monster into the garage. I was going to try to salvage some of the wood from it. It's solid oak, almost four inches thick solid oak. Let's take a look."

It takes them almost half an hour to locate the door in the garage and then drag it out into a shady spot on the patio. Both are drenched in sweat by the time they are set to examine it. Gabby then retrieves some tools and the two begin poking around looking for something that resembles a hole that someone might have drilled, other than the peep hole.

Glenn tries to unscrew one of the hinges, but layers of varnish have filled in the slots on the screws and his screw driver cannot get a grip.

"Watch and learn, Padawan," Gabby says as she uses the edge of her screw driver tip to plow out the varnish by holding it at an angle and tapping gently on the handle with a hammer. Once the varnish is removed, she is able to easily turn the large wood screw.

Following her example, Glenn cleans the varnish from each screw slot and then removes them. The door is so massive that it has four sets of hinges, but under the second one from the top they find a two-inch-in-diameter hole neatly drilled where the hinge plate covers it.

Using a pair of needle nose pliers, Glenn extracts a rolled up piece of paper. The once-white paper has faded to a light tan on the outside of the roll, and there is a brittleness to the paper that forces them to work together to gently unroll it. There they find handwritten:

To whoever finds this note: I hope that you are remodeling this lovely house. We have lived here for almost twenty years and have come to feel deeply about it. We wept when I had to put big bolts in this door to hold the cross bars. Each year the weather has worn away the beautiful finish on the outside, but we dare not touch it. It is our hope that you will love Babcook Manor as much as we, but that you'll be able to take better care of it. John & Mary Galway.

"This has nothing to do with all of the other clues," Glenn observes after several minutes pass in silence.

"This is a love note to the house. Do you suppose that's where he's been going all along?"

"But then why play us with all those clues about his past activities while using Presidential assassination-related clues?"

143

Chapter 42

Once they lug the massive oak door back into the garage and put away the tools, the two sit down on the patio trying to decide their next move. Gabby is about to get more iced tea for them when Glenn asks, "Did you ever look at the attic of the house? That Gianni dude said that there is supposed to be money hidden here. Maybe Galway put a false wall up there, too."

"I insulated the attic spaces when I did the renovations, but did not notice anything out of the ordinary. Though I have to admit that I was not looking for false walls and I did miss the one in the garage. It's worth a try," shrugs Gabby.

They go back into the garage, pick up a ladder, flashlights, a few tools and Gabby's tool belt, complete with the .45. Finding the attic access hole in the closet of the master bedroom, they push up the cover, getting a shower of pink insulation in the process. Once up into the extremely hot and humid attic, Gabby heads for the west gable end while Glenn moves cautiously along the single 2x12s that form a walkway toward the east end.

Both the east and west gable ends prove to be authentic. Gabby moans, "We're sweating putty balls up here. I'm going to be drenched before we get out. Can you see any place else to look?"

"No," Glenn responds as he looks around. "Wait, what about the attic space over the turret?" He points to his left.

"I never got into that space as I could not find an opening," Gabby calls as she starts stepping along two parallel joists that lead toward the turret. There are no boards for walkways heading in that direction.

"Well, looky here," Gabby yells in excitement. "There is an access point, but it is cleverly disguised. I've been at this too long. Now I see such things as hidden doors that I never noticed before. Weird."

As soon as Glenn brings the tools they begin removing nails. Once the cover is free they lay it aside. There, in plain view, are neat stacks of brick sized bundles, each bundle wrapped in Visqueen.

Glenn crawls inside the turret attic and throws out four of the bundles. Sitting down on the cover of the opening, they each take a bundle and trying to keep their sweat from dripping onto the surface, they remove the plastic wraps. After a few minutes counting they conclude that each bundle contains $10,000 in cash—mostly in $50s. They count 56 bundles in the hiding spot. One of Gabby's bundles contains bills that have not been in circulation for forty years.

"Is any of that old money any good today?" Glenn asks.

"Don't know. I'll do some checking on the Internet tomorrow at work. I suppose they'd have some value to collectors. Might even be worth more than their face value."

"How could you spend this? Aren't there regulations about deposits of cash over a certain amount?"

"Yes, I think in the range of $10,000 before the DEA or somebody has to be notified by the bank."

"What if you just report finding it? Which is what we did."

"If it is determined that this money was the proceeds of some illegal activity, then it would be confiscated and that would be the end of it."

"Well, since we've pretty much decided that Galway was a hit man, then this has to be blood money."

Gabby looks at her hands and the cash she has unwrapped. *Out, out damned spot* runs through her mind. She re-wraps the money and then throws the bundles back onto the pile. Glenn does the same with his two bundles. Sopping wet with sweat they carefully replace the access hatch, leaving all of the cash as they found it.

Yet another reason for Gabby to lie awake at night— blood money in the attic.

Chapter 43

One week to the day after the blood money was found, Gabby's cell phone rings shortly after 3:30 AM. Rolling over from a fitful sleep she looks at her phone to see the time and notes the caller is Community Care Haven.

"Hello."

"This is Helen Patterson, administrator at The Haven. I am calling for Gabriel Gordon."

"Speaking."

"Miss Gordon, I am calling about John Galway. I am afraid there has been a terrible tragedy. Can you come here immediately?"

"Why? What has happened? Is Galway dead?"

"Yes. He... he... he's been shot I'm afraid."

"He was WHAT?"

"Someone shot him through the window of his room. The police and coroner are here now. We thought you would like to make the arrangements for him once the coroner is finished, and the police would like to talk to you."

By now Gabby is fully awake and trying to shuck off her sweat pants while holding on to the phone. "I'll be there in fifteen minutes," is her response as she drops the phone on the bed.

Twelve minutes later as she nears the nursing home on Galena Avenue, Gabby can see numerous police cars blocking off the streets leading to The Haven. She has just finished a hurried call to Glenn when a police officer waves her to a stop. A conversation with the female officer results in a check on Gabby's status with someone through the officer's radio. Soon Gabby is in the Haven's parking lot.

At the main entrance to the nursing home she again has to get clearance to enter what is now a crime scene. Helen Patterson meets Gabby at the door and escorts her to the lounge area near the door to Galway's room. All the lights in the lounge area are on, the bright fluorescents casting a stark, blue hue on the surroundings. The glare brings Gabby to the reality of the situation as Galway's death stares her in the face.

A tall, muscular man dressed in a polo shirt and slacks, a pistol and badge on his belt, comes over to Gabby.

"I'm Mark Sumner, Freeport Police Department. I'm heading the investigation into the death of John Galway. You are his attorney?"

"Yes. My name is Gabriel Gordon. I'm from Weston and Sanderson." With that, she hands Sumner her business card. "Cell number is on the back."

"Thank you. Do you know if Mr. Galway has any family?"

"He has a sister in Florida, but they have not spoken in many, many years. She believes he is already dead and he wanted to keep it that way. And by the way, John Galway is an alias. His real name was Sean Michael Fallon. Spelled S-E-A-N-M-I-C-H-A-E-L-F-A-L-L-O-N."

"And you know this how?"

"When he had me prepare a Power of Attorney document he had me list both names." Detective Sumner looks at Helen Patterson with raised eyebrows.

"We did not know that. Only recently did Miss Gordon suggest there might be some things wrong with what we had been told by Mr. Galway. We have no Social Security number for him, either."

"Do either of you know anything else about him? Wife, etc.?"

Gabby responds, "His wife is deceased, about two years ago. They were both living here at the time. She was suffering from Alzheimer's. They were both from Chicago."

"Did they move into The Haven from Chicago?"

"No," Gabby continues. "They were living at Babcook Manor from about nineteen-sixty-three till two-thousand-three as near as I can piece together."

"I grew up in Freeport," Detective Sumner notes, "we always thought that place was deserted."

"They lived in the basement and almost never left in those forty years. There is a report in your files of an incident

147

when Mrs. Galway ran out onto River Road one night. That led
to her being placed here and he came along."

"Was Mr. Galway, or Fallon, or whoever…was he
suffering from Alzheimer's?"

"Yes," Helen responds at the same time Gabby says,
"No." Sumner looks back and forth between the two women
awaiting an explanation.

"He faked the dementia in order to say near his wife,"
Gabby finally offers.

"What?" Peterson exclaims. Not only is she facing the
fact that one of her residents has been murdered, but now she is
discovering that he had been living here under a false
diagnosis.

"Did he get many visitors?"

"I can check the logs," Peterson says softly, her self-
control bordering on the brink of collapse, "but I am certain
that he never had a visitor the entire time he was here. Except,
of course, for Miss Gordon."

"There's Jack Bruce," Gabby notes.

"Who?" Sumner and Peterson ask simultaneously.

"A man who brought Galway his mail from a Post
Office box every Monday," Gabby explains. "I spoke with Mr.
Bruce a few weeks ago. He has been working for Galway for
the past thirty years, first hauling groceries and packages to
Babcook and then making mail runs here."

"I know a Jack Bruce. Elderly black man who drives a
nicely-restored seventy-six Caddy. Great guy," Sumner
concludes.

"That's him," Gabby assures.

"He must never have signed in," mumbles Peterson as
she sees further flaws in her system.

"Can you think of why anyone would want to kill Mr.
Galway?"

"Just last weekend he revealed to me that his bank
account was missing over four million dollars and that he
thought it was the work of someone in a law firm in Chicago
charged with managing his assets. That's why he hired me to
begin looking after his affairs."

"Did you say 'four million'?" the incredulous detective queries.

"Yes. The account is in a Swiss bank, Credit Suisse. That's spelled C-R-E-D-I-T-S-U-I-S-S-E," Gabby adds as Sumner writes down the bank's name.

"Well, then there is certainly a motive for murder."

Just as the detective is about to ask another question, two EMTs, one with the name "Jay" on his name tag, come out of Galway's room. They stop where Gabby, Helen and the detective are standing.

"Mark, do you want us to stay around until the funeral home comes to remove the body?" Jay inquires.

"Won't be necessary. The coroner is here and we'll stay until the body has been removed. Which funeral home?"

"Who handled Mrs. Galway's arrangements?" Gabby asks.

"Burke-Tubbs," replies Helen. "I already called them since their name was on Galway's, err...whoever-he-was's record."

"That's fine. I'll contact them about the final arrangements," Gabby says to everyone standing there. After the EMTs leave, Gabby asks, "How did someone get in here with all of the alarms?"

"It appears that the shooter climbed the fence into the courtyard between the wings of the building and then shot through the window," Sumner responds.

"The sound must have scared everyone to death."

"The shooter probably used a silencer or sound suppressor. No one seems to have heard a thing," the detective expands.

"A CNA on her hourly rounds found him slumped over in his wheelchair, which is where he always slept," Helen adds. "It was only when she tried to sit him upright that she saw the blood on his chest. Funny thing, he always sat facing that window, like he knew someone might be out there." With that Helen goes over and drops into a chair. She is visibly shaking.

"Do you know what Galway did for a living?" the detective asks.

"Supposed to have been a consultant of some sort. I have been trying to get a clear picture of his life, but he was not very talkative."

"Well, he'll be even less help now. If we have more questions, we'll be in touch. Mrs. Paterson? We'll leave an officer inside here to keep people out of the room and another to keep anyone out of the court yard. The State Crime Lab personnel will be here in an hour or so to fully process the scene."

"If it can be arranged, we would ask that they be in plain clothes so as not to alarm the residents. Most of them have slept through all of this and I don't want to cause undue stress."

"I'll arrange for that. If we have any more questions for you, will you be in your office today?" Sumner concludes.

Chapter 44

It is in the early morning hours of Sunday, June 29, 2010 that Galway is killed. On Monday morning Gabby goes to the funeral home. The people at Burke-Tubbs are solicitous, not knowing the complete nature of Gabby's relationship with Galway. She has them follow the same procedures they used for Mary Alice. Cremation, and then the ashes are to be interred next to hers in a plot in a small rural cemetery on Browns Mill Road.

There is no headstone for Mrs. Galway so the funeral home asks if there will be one placed for the two of them. Gabby tells them she will think about it and get back to them. The death notice in the *Journal Standard* contains the same basic information as Mrs. Galway's obit, but the murder makes front page headlines.

Glenn comes down to Freeport on Tuesday morning, and it is just the two of them at the graveside when Galway's urn is lowered into the ground. Although Galway and his wife were married in the Catholic Church, Gabby is uncertain as to his recent relationship with the Church. Deciding that it will be better to have clergy present than not, she has a Deacon from St. Thomas present to conduct a funeral service. After the brief funeral Glenn heads back to work and Gabby does the same.

Later that afternoon Gabby asks Sam and one of the other attorneys in the office, Kallen Moorsman, to witness her opening the envelope she had been given by Galway the last time she saw him alive. The envelope is marked "To be opened in the event of my death" and signed by Galway. Inside is a one page document in Galway's scrawling handwriting.

I, John Galway, do declare this to be my last will and testament. I declare that the other will I signed is no longer valid. I declare Gabriel Gordon as executor of my estate and I also leave to her for her personal use in the upkeep and care of Babcook Manor the following: 1) the contents of a safety deposit box at State Bank, Freeport; 2) the residue of my *account at Credit Suisse; 3) the residue of my account at Union Bank of Switzerland, not mentioned in my prior will, subject to the following: that after all my medical, nursing home and funeral expenses are paid, then the remainder of the funds be distributed as follows: A grave marker listing Sean Michael Fallon ~ died 201__ and Mary Alice Fallon ~ died 2008; the sum of three dollars ($3.00) to my sister, Mary Catherine Shaughnessy who lives in Naples, Florida; and the sum of $300,000.00 (three hundred thousand dollars) to Community Care Haven, Freeport.*

The document is signed by Fallon and then witnessed by two people whom Gabby assumes are Haven employees. Both added statements in their own hand writing that Galway had written the Will in their presence and that he was coherent and knowledgeable of his surroundings, of the date and other relevant facts at the time he wrote and signed the document.

"Holy, shit! Ooops. Sorry, Gabby." Sam exclaims. "Like that's a hell of a chunk of cash for a nursing home. They must have taken super care of him."

"He must have really hated his sister," Kallen adds. "The nursing home gets three hundred grand and she gets a measly three bucks. Talk about an insult,"

"He did have a deep dislike for his sister. He said she thought he was dead and he wanted to keep it that way. I'd guess getting a check from a brother she thought was dead will be the real shock. The amount of the check may be immaterial."

After signing statements that they have witnessed Gabby opening the Will, Kallen and Sam leave Gabby's office. Then Gabby finds a small piece of paper still in the Will's envelope. Pulling it out she sees that the folded sheet has "For G. Gordon—personal" written on it, again in Galway's hand writing. The note inside reads, *To find the final answer, make the connections: Freeport, TR, TNT, RR, PWJ.*

"What the hell is that supposed to mean?" Gabby asks out loud.

Chapter 45

After reading Galway's Will, Gabby drives out to State Bank. Her errand could have been done on the phone, but Gabby needs to get out of her office just to clear her mind of all that has happened in the past few days. Once at the bank, speaking to the vice-president, Marie Coeur, Gabby reports that Galway/Fallon is dead and that his safety deposit box needs to be sealed until the court confirms her status as executor.

"I know you monitor the death notices, but I did not know if you would catch the Fallon name in conjunction with Galway," Gabby explains.

"We caught the name in both the obituaries and the front page. We don't have many murders in Freeport."

"Well, thank you for your time. I'll be in touch when the court approves my status."

Just as she turns to leave, Gabby spots Scurry coming into the lobby. Turning to Coeur, Gabby says that someone has just shown up who might try to gain access to Galway's box. Coeur agrees to allow Gabby to be present when Coeur talks to Scurry. A quick phone call to the receptionist has Scurry escorted to Coeur's office. It is a very shocked Scurry who walks through the door and sees Gabby standing there.

"Miss Gordon. What are you doing here?"

"I might ask you the same."

"On business." Turning to Coeur, Scurry switches on his charm and asks to have the safety deposit box of John Galway. He produces a key to the box.

"I'm sorry, Mr. ...?"

"Scurry, Sean. I am Mr. Galway's attorney," comes a reply through a smile that could have melted rock.

"Well, I'm sorry, Mr. Sean. That box has been sealed pending a court order."

"It's Scurry. As I noted, I am Mr. Galway's attorney and I am unaware of any legal proceedings concerning my client that would warrant the sealing of his safety deposit box."

"It seems, Mr. Scurry, that someone has murdered your client and pending a court-appointed executor of his estate, we legally cannot allow anyone access."

"But I am the executor for Mr. Galway's Will."

"That must be decided by the court," Gabby cuts in.

"I have a copy of his Will with me, if you wish to see it."

"Do you always travel around with copies of clients' Wills in your briefcase?"

"Uhhh…well, when I left the office to drive out here, I…I…grabbed the Galway file, not thinking what else it contained beyond the information on his safety deposit box. But irregardless of why I have the Will, I am the executor so I need access to that box."

"What is the date on the Will you have?" Gabby queries.

"What difference does that make?"

"Because I have a copy of a Will signed by Galway that was created less than a week ago. Unless you have one dated since then, mine makes yours moot."

"And it doesn't matter whose has what Will, until we get a court order granting someone executor status, we cannot allow anyone access to the box," Coeur states with enough force that the discussion is obviously ended.

As Scurry turns to leave he hisses at Gabby with a sneer, "I'll see you in court." With that he stomps out of the office. Gabby says to no one in particular, "It must be tough these days to be an attorney in Chicago who wears such expensive suits and then has to get them wrinkled while driving all the way out to Freeport."

Coeur maintains her professional demeanor and refrains from responding.

Chapter 46

It is close to four that afternoon when documents are delivered to Gabby at her office notifying her that a suit has been filed in Circuit Court contesting the Will of John Galway now in her possession. Chief Judge Alma Crockett has set a hearing for ten the next morning. *Hmmmm* Gabby thinks, *Scurry must have some clout with the Chief Judge or he threw a hissy fit to get a hearing on such short notice.*

Gabby appears as requested in Judge Crockett's courtroom at 10:00 AM the next morning. Also present are Jack Wilson, attorney for State Bank, which is named in the suit for some odd reason, and Sean Scurry. As they sit there in silence waiting for the judge, Gabby notices that Scurry is wearing the same suit, shirt and tie as the day before, only they are even more wrinkled.

Wilson, who was sitting next to Gabby, observes that she is looking at Scurry's clothing. He writes on her yellow legal pad, "Custom-made, two-button, gray pinstripe, probably virgin wool." The exchange between Gabby and Wilson that follows is done on the same notepad:

Gabby: "$$?"

Wilson: "Suit = $1,500, shirt = $150. Not real top line for custom. That's why it's so wrinkled."

Gabby: "What constitutes 'top line'?"

Wilson: "North of $10,000. Scurry is trying to look the part of a custom suit high roller, but his pocketbook must be closer to upscale off-the-rack. The fit suggests custom-made, but the quality of the fabric is at the lower end of the scale."

Gabby: "How do you know so much about men's suits?"

Wilson: "I'm on the Ill. Bar Assoc. Exec. Committee. Some of the attorney's I meet there would put Scurry to shame when it comes to conspicuous sartorial splendor."

The mini-lesson in higher-end men's clothing abruptly comes to a halt when the Court Reporter enters, and the Bailiff announces the Judge as everyone stands. Judge Alma Crockett, at a few inches over five feet, has jet black hair and a stare that could induce any species of animal to voluntarily move further down the food chain.

"In the matter of the Estate of John Galway, for the record who is present?"

"Sean Scurry for the law firm of Hoban, Boylan, Doran, and Malloy of Chicago, Your Honor, the Plaintiff." Scurry pronounces the name of his firm as if he is announcing the entrance of royalty at a palace ball.

"Ahh, yes, Mr. Scurry. The personal request of an old friend, Jack Garrity, Chief Justice from the Appellate Court, has gotten you this hearing on such very short notice, especially on the day before a long holiday weekend. I'm giving up time with my grandchildren, so I trust all this fuss will be worth the effort."

Next Gabby and Jack Wilson introduce themselves.

Without any further preliminaries, Judge Crockett begins, "Well Mr. Scurry, I have to admit that in my twenty-three years in the judicial system I have never had a petition delivered in handwritten form. Is your firm long on partners and short on secretaries?"

"I beg your pardon, Your Honor," Scurry begins as he stands. "Since my firm is in Chicago and I did not have access to assistance when preparing the petition, I was forced to resort to such informality." With that he begins to pace back and forth behind his table. Gabby notes that he has his right hand in his pants pocket fingering coins.

"For the record, Mr. Scurry, this county's name is spelled S-T-E-P-H-E-N-S-O-N. It's on the outside of the building. Not S-T-E-V-E-N-S-O-N. And, even out here on the frontier we have FAX machines."

"My apology, Your Honor." The pacing continues, as does the coin rattling.

"Mr. Scurry?"

"Your Honor?"

"Please have a seat."

"Thank you, Your Honor."

"Now correct me if I'm wrong, Mr. Scurry." At the mention of his name, Scurry is up and pacing again, coins rattling.

"Please sit down, counselor."

"Yes ma'am. I mean Your Honor."

"What the Plaintiff is asking is that the Will of John Galway as presented by the Plaintiff be declared the rightful document for the execution of Mr. Galway's estate. Is that a fair summary, Mr. Scurry?"

"May it please the court, Your Honor," Scurry begins as he again rises and resumes pacing and jingling. "We believe that the document which Miss Gordon has offered is either a forgery or coerced from my client."

"Your Honor," Gabby interjects.

"Ms. Gordon. And Mr. Scurry, please sit."

"Your Honor, Mr. Galway wrote the document dated 26 June 2010 in his own hand and we can produce the two individuals who witnessed him writing it and then signing it in their presence. I was neither there at the time he prepared his Will, nor was I aware that he planned to do so at that time. In addition, I was not aware that he had a prior Will. And I wish it to be noted that when I met with Mr. Scurry in his office less than a month ago, he contended that he had never heard of John Galway and refused to discuss whether or not his law firm managed a trust for someone of that name."

"Mr. Scurry, is that correct?"

"Uhh. Uhh. Well, uhh, she came to see me regarding…"

"Opposing Counsel, Mr. Scurry."

"Sorry, Your Honor. Opposing Counsel came to see me regarding the Flaherty Family Trust, and I was not prepared for her questions about Mr. Galway," Scurry whines as he wags his index finger at Gabby.

"Miss Gordon, is that correct?"

"Your Honor, they are all connected. John Galway's wife was Mary Alice Flaherty, and as such a party to the Flaherty Family Trust."

"She was what?" Scurry shouts as he again jumps to his feet. "You're making that up!" he adds this time accompanied by deliberately shaking a finger at Gabby.

"Mr. Scurry, in my courtroom one does not accuse Opposing Counsel of 'making that up' unless one has substantial proof. Are you prepared to offer such proof?"

"This is all bogus. She conned that old man..."

"Mr. Scurry, I will tolerate neither outbursts nor unsubstantiated claims. You did not answer my question." After a moment's thought, Judge Crockett continues, "Mr. Scurry when was the last time you litigated a case?"

"Sorry, Your Honor, I'm a little rusty on courtroom procedures. It has been eighteen years since I argued a case."

"And how long have you been practicing law, Mr. Scurry?"

"Uhhh... eighteen years, Your Honor. You see, one of the junior associates from my firm was supposed to be here to handle this, but he must be uhhh...well, caught in traffic."

"What sort of law do you practice, may I ask?"

"I handle trusts, estates and wills. Trusts, mostly."

"And you've never been in a courtroom?"

"Oh, yes, but my firm has specialists who do the oral arguments. I advise and observe, Your Honor."

"But I take it you've not observed too closely?"

"Apparently not, Your Honor."

As the judge turns back to the documents, the door of the courtroom opens as Georgie Steinmur stumbles in. At four feet, ten inches, with a bald pate and thick horn-rimmed glasses, George R. Steinmur is at the bottom of the legal pecking order in Stephenson County and the general butt of most legal humor. Relegated to mostly DUI and accident cases, Georgie as he is known, married into one of the richest families in the county, making his legal practice mostly a hobby, which is fortunate considering his lack of legal acumen.

"Counselor Steinmur, are you in the wrong courtroom?" the Judge asks.

"No, Your Honor. I am here in the matter of the Will of Sean M. Fallon."

"This is a hearing on the Will of John Galway."

"Your Honor," Gabby interjects. "John Galway and Sean M. Fallon are one in the same. Galway was an alias under which Fallon lived for at least forty years."

"Oh, get real. You're making that up, too!" Scurry exclaims as he again jumps to his feet.

"Mr. Scurry, be seated! Now, Mr. Steinmur, whom do you represent in this case?"

Looking at the note in his hand to make sure of the name, Georgie responds, "Mrs. Mary Catherine Shaughnessy, sister of Mr. Fallon, er Galway." As he is speaking Georgie approaches the bench to show the judge his telephone message to verify his statement.

"There is no need for me to see that, Mr. Steinmur," Judge Crockett says as she waves him away. "Is Mrs. Shaughnessy present?"

"No, Your Honor. My office received a call from her this morning. She lives in Florida and is willing to come here if needed to testify."

"How did she happen to pick your law firm?"

"I think she told my secretary that after she saw the death notice on the Internet, she found my name in the online Yellow Pages. She said something about it sounding Jewish so she thought that would help."

After a pause to regain her composure, Judge Crockett continues, "Well, what we have are two Wills, one dated in nineteen sixty-two and naming Mr. Scurry's law firm as Executor and one written just a week ago naming Ms. Gordon as Executor. Both Wills specifically leave to your client, Mr. Steinmur, the princely sum of three dollars."

"I beg your pardon; did Your Honor say three dollars?"

"Yes, Counselor, three dollars. Both Wills are very specific."

"Won't collect much of a fee for that payout," George murmurs under his breath as he drops into a seat in the area for the general public.

"You Honor," Gabby says as she rises. "Mr. Galway, and we would like stipulate that we refer to him as Galway for

159

the sake of clarity in these proceedings, told me that his sister
thought that he was dead and that he wanted to keep it that
way. We can produce other witnesses who will testify to such
statements by Mr. Galway. I surmised that theirs was not a
cordial relationship."

"It would seem so, Miss Gordon. And, yes, for the sake
of clarity the Court will stipulate that John Galway and Sean
Michael Fallon are one and the same and that for these
proceedings John Galway will be the preferred name unless
Opposing Counsel objects."

Scurry jumps to his feet, "All this is wasting time I
don't care if Galway left his sister three dollars or three
thousand dollars. Both Wills agree on her status, but this issue
of the …"

"Mr. Scurry, I am going to hold you in contempt of
court if you continue these outbursts. And, Mr. Scurry, you
have not responded to Ms. Gordon's motion to stipulate that
John Galway and Sean Fallon are one and the same person."

"Your Honor, I-I-I…" Scurry stammers. "I have no
objection… at this time."

"The Court agrees to the stipulation regarding John
Galway and Sean Fallon being one and the same person. Now,
Mr. Wilson, what is your purpose in being here?"

"Your guess is as good as mine, Your Honor. State
Bank was named in the complaint, so here I am."

"Mr. Scurry, is there a particular reason you named
State Bank in your complaint?"

"Yeah. They would not grant me access to Mr.
Galway's safety deposit box, a safety deposit box to which I
am entitled to have access."

"Your Honor."

"Oh, sorry, Your Honor…Your Honor"

"Illinois law provides that the safety deposit boxes of a
deceased person be sealed until the courts have appointed an
Executor to examine the contents for the purpose of
determining the total assets of the estate."

"But I have power of attorney."

"Your Honor."

"Your Honor, sorry, Your Honor."

"It must be some strange form of Illinois law they practice in Chicago, Mr. Scurry. Out here power of attorney terminates at death."

"Oh, sorry, Your Honor. That fact seems to have slipped my mind."

Before Judge Crockett can ask another question the door of the courtroom opens and Assistant State's Attorney Terry Ryan walks in. He moves into the space between where the opposing attorneys are seated. Ryan is tall, thin and has the face of a youth who ought to still be in high school.

"Well, are we having a meeting of the county bar association in here this morning, Mr. Ryan?" the Judge asks with a large degree of sarcasm.

Looking around at the four other attorneys in the room, Ryan, a man with no sense of humor, shrugs slightly and turns back to address the court. "Your Honor, the State's Attorney's office has received notification from the Cook County State's Attorney that they are investigating the law firm of Hoban, Boylan, Doran, and Malloy of Chicago for improprieties in the handling of a trust fund for a John Galway, a/k/a Sean Fallon. If I am not mistaken, that is the case before you?"

"Well, Mr. Scurry, this just gets more interesting by the minute. I suppose next we'll discover that someone involved in this case is also accused of starting the Chicago Fire. Mr. Ryan, can you provide the court with any further information regarding this investigation?"

"It seems that a Mary Helen Hannigan, a secretary with the firm, has disappeared along with funds from the trust fund of Mr. Galway."

"That old bitch!" spits Scurry.

"Mr. Scurry, you are about to find yourself an unwilling guest of our new county jail. Does the Cook County State's Attorney offer any ideas as to where this lady has gone or how much is missing?"

"No, Your Honor."

"I might be able to help, Your Honor," Gabby offers. "Mr. Galway stated that his account was missing over five

161

million dollars. Further, Your Honor, I was informed by a
Chicago police detective that Mary Helen Hannigan has fled to
a jurisdiction that does not have extradition to the United
States."

"An interesting set of facts," intones Ryan and with that
he abruptly turns and leaves the courtroom.

Silence follows as Judge Crockett examines the
documents before her. Scurry gets back to his feet and begins
to pace and jingle, but the Judge stares him back into his seat.

At length the Judge issues her ruling: "The Court sees
no reason to consider the nineteen-sixty-two Will to have any
precedence over the more recent Will. That being said, and
given the nature of the untimely death of Mr. Galway/Fallon,
Miss Gordon is granted Executor status pro tem. Given the
nature of the on-going police investigations in Cook County
and the nature of Mr. Galway's death, the Court will give leave
to the Plaintiff to move for a re-examination of Counselor
Gordon's status should extenuating circumstances come to
light. Further, the Court directs Miss Gordon and Mr. Wilson,
along with a representative from the Stephenson County State's
Attorney's office and the Freeport Police Department to
immediately open the safety deposit box of Mr. Galway at
State Bank, inventory the contents, and then report said
inventory to both law enforcement agencies involved, as well
as to this Court for purposes of Probate."

"I should be part of that committee," Scurry shouts as
he again jumps to his feet.

"Mr. Scurry, this court has had it with your outbursts.
Consider this your final warning. Given the nature of the
investigation of your law firm, I see no reason to grant you
access to that deposit box or anything else connected with Mr.
Galway. In addition the Court notes that the Will presented by
the Plaintiff names the law firm of Hoban, Boylan, Doran, and
Malloy as executors. Pending some authorization from that
firm, you personally, Mr. Scurry, have no direct claim to the
power of Executor. Miss Gordon, your office will supply Mr.
Scurry's firm with a copy of the inventory of the box. Court is
recessed in this matter until Miss Gordon is set to proceed with

probating the Will or the Plaintiff has further evidence for the Court to consider."

Chapter 47

That afternoon the "committee" appointed by Judge Crockett assembles to open Galway's safety deposit box. At the suggestion of Detective Sumner, all are wearing vinyl gloves provided by the police.

Once the box is opened they find the following: 1) a large, cylindrical object which Gabby assumes but does not say aloud could be the missing silencer for the sniper rifle; 2) a set of papers dated 2001 giving details on how to access an account online as well as the necessary PIN at United Bank of Switzerland; 3) a codicil also dated 2001 to a set of papers establishing an account at Credit Suisse, along with a 1960 letter from Fallon to the Hoban, Boylan, Doran, and Malloy law firm granting them access to the account for the purposes of paying all submitted expenses for John and Mary Alice Galway; 4) a copy of the Will and the subsequent 1960 estate settlement for Michael Joseph Flaherty leaving his daughter Mary Alice Flaherty Fallon the sum of $4 million; and 5) the old Will of Mary Alice and Sean M. Fallon as drawn up by Hoban, Boylan, Doran, and Malloy in 1962.

Ryan restates that his office will convey the inventory list, sans the account numbers and PINs to Cook County authorities. Gabby duly notes she will do the same for Hoban, Boylan, Doran, and Malloy. Again, without the account numbers and PINs.

When she gets back to her office, Gabby checks the status of the Union Bank of Switzerland account, finding a balance on $12,592,402.37. According to the account's history, except for the quarterly addition of interest, there have been no transactions since it was opened in 1960.

Chapter 48

Even though they have spent hours each evening talking on the phone, Gabby is still happy to see Glenn when he arrives just before lunchtime on Thursday, the day after the hearing. After a light lunch they go over to the Manor to wander around its empty rooms while they discuss all the events which have led them to the current situation.

"If Galway was so worried about his life that he slept sitting in a wheelchair facing a window for the last eight years, and that was after living in the basement of this place for the better part of forty years, what the hell did he do that was so bad?" Glenn demands.

"Maybe he was just paranoid."

"There's paranoia and then there's paranoia. His wife went along with it, so she must have seen some validity to his fears."

"Assuming the fear was rational, he had to have whacked someone of major significance. Can you fire up that fancy cell phone slash laptop your firm just bought for all its architects?" Gabby queries.

"Sure, I've got reception here so I can go on-line, but what am I looking for?"

"See if there is some website that lists deaths of important or famous people by year. If Galway shot someone that important, then maybe it'll show up in the headlines."

"What year we looking for?"

"Nineteen-sixty-two seems to be the best place to start. That's just before they arrived here."

"Well, there are some possibilities, but none that make sense. Even if he was working for the CIA at the time."

"Well, move up to '63."

After a few minutes of search, Glenn mutters under his breath, "Geez Louise Gertrude!" Then he hands Gabby his phone.

The screen shows the headline from November 22, 1963, "President Assassinated!"

Gabby slumps back against the wall of the living room where they have been talking. She slowly slides down the wall to the floor where she sits in silence. Glenn sits down next to her as the magnitude of what they may have uncovered slowly sinks in. The quiet lasts over ten minutes as each seeks to process the gravity of the revelation linked to all the clues Galway has given them.

"Maybe it's just a coincidence," Gabby whispers finally.

"Rule 39—there's no such thing as coincidence."

"What? Who's rule?"

"Gibbs. Come on girl, you've never watched NCIS?"

"I have never, ever owned a TV."

"We'll have to remedy that. Besides, I've already broken Rule 15."

"Rule 15?"

"Never, ever involve a lawyer." With that he kisses Gabby on the cheek.

Gabby shrugs and weakly smiles, too preoccupied with the idea of the Kennedy assassination to give much thought to Glenn's TV allusion. Then they fall back into silence staring out the front window and at the road down by the river. As time passes Glenn complains that his butt is aching from sitting on the hardwood floor. As he shifts his weight from one side to the other Gabby asks, "You noticed that silver car across the road? It's been there since we sat down."

"Never noticed it 'til now. Darkened windows so you can't tell if anyone's in there. You getting paranoid, too?"

Glenn runs his hands through his thick black hair as he looks up at the ceiling in thought. After a couple of seconds he comments, almost as if to himself, "I can't believe this escaped me 'til now. When I was in high school I was a geek when it came to the Kennedy assassination."

"Oh, so you're not a geek today, Mr. AIA architect who spends weekends on road trips to look at old houses?"

"OK, point you. But it did lead me to you—that's not such a bad thing, so point me. But I did read and re-read every book that was written on the assassination. I still have them at my parents' home."

"Were you convinced there was a conspiracy?"

"At first I was totally into the whole conspiracy thing. But as time went on and I became a more rational thinker who could carefully weigh evidence and sources, I became less and less so. Most of the theories were based on acceptance of some pieces of evidence that supported that particular theory and the rest were dismissed, usually with very little rationale. But the Warren Commission report left more questions than answers, so the conspiracy seeds began to sprout before the ink was even dry on its final report."

"I recall that the Mafia was the subject of at least one of those theories. Certainly Galway had connections, at least to organized criminals in Chicago."

"He also had ties to the CIA, which was another favorite villain of some conspiracy nuts."

"Correct me if I'm wrong, but IF, granting that Oswald was not the killer, IF there was some group—Mafia, CIA, Cubans, whoever—behind the assassination, then whoever pulled the trigger would want to disappear forever."

"That's assuming that the killer was a professional hit man. Anyone acting alone who was some sort of nut would want to be known for the kill. But, back to a professional, I would think that if I was some Mafia kingpin or CIA chief who wanted the President whacked, then I would take pains after the fact to have everyone in the chain of command killed off as soon as possible. You would not want anyone left who could finger you as the person who ordered it, especially if they could be coerced to do so years later as part of a plea agreement for some other crime."

"Maybe no one really ordered a hit. Like that English king who asked the rhetorical question about someone ridding him of a troublesome priest and those knights who overheard the king and went out and killed Thomas à Beckett just to please him. Some mid-level guy hears his boss complain about JFK, so he decides to go off on his own to earn a quick promotion."

"That assumes that the mid-level dude has the deep pockets to finance the hit. Anyone contemplating such an assassination would hire the best and the best would know that if he made the hit, it would be his last. So, he'd want a big chunk of change so he had something to live on the rest of his life, probably on some obscure island."

"Hence Swiss bank accounts. And if he feared that he'd get whacked himself, then finding a place to hide out for say, fifty years would be another necessity. But maybe it would be safer to hide where they would never to think to look for you—some small city in the Midwest. Sort of a do-it-yourself witness protection program."

"But all we have is circumstantial evidence. The date on the *Tribune* slip and the approximate year when Galway arrived here are the only things that point to Kennedy. All the rest could have been related to some rival gang chief getting hit or who knows who."

"What we need," continues Gabby after a pause "is to place Galway at the scene of the crime."

Chapter 49

After thinking in silence about all they've discussed, Glenn finally moans, "I'm famished. Let's go rustle up some grub."

They decide to go to Amigos for dinner. The silver Chrysler 200 is still parked across the road when they leave for the restaurant, and they observe a well-tanned runner heading east on River Road. When they returned, a silver Chrysler 200 is again there, but in a different location, and the same runner is heading west, his grey t-shirt soaked with sweat. Gabby mentions that the same car is there, but Glenn says it is not the same car.

"How do you know it's a different car?"

"Same color, make and model, but different numbers on the license plates."

"You memorized the plate numbers?"

"No, but I have a habit of adding license plate numbers in my head to reduce them to their lowest number. That one is a six, the one there when we left was a three."

"You do what?"

"Add numbers. Take a plate number like on your car," Glenn says as he points to Gabby's Wrangler as they walk past the garage. Five two zero six six eight nine. Five plus two is seven. Seven plus zero is seven. Seven plus six is thirteen. Take the thirteen, add the one plus the three and you get four. Four plus six is ten, which reduces to one. One plus eight is nine, and nine plus nine is eighteen. One plus eight is nine. You're a nine."

"But I always wanted to be a ten."

"Well, you're a ten plus to me, but your plate number reduces to nine."

"And you do this because?"

"Started doing it to occupy my mind on long drives and to keep in practice doing simple math in my head. The car that was here when we left was a three and the one out there now is a six. If it's the same car, then someone changed the plates."

Gabby just shakes her head as she walks over to the patio and flops down on a lounge chair.

Chapter 50

It is almost half past nine when they sit down on the patio. The heat of the day has begun to abate as they sit there silently staring off into the deepening twilight.

"He would have wanted to get to Dallas and back without calling attention to himself," Gabby finally suggests aloud. "Flying would probably have been out, especially since he'd want his favorite sniper rifle. Even in nineteen-sixty-three taking a rifle on a commercial airliner would have attracted attention, especially on the flight back after the president had been assassinated."

"What if whoever ordered the hit provided a private plane?"

"Possible, but again, you'd want to minimize the number of people in the chain that linked the shooter and the bigwig who ordered the hit. Private planes and so forth create too many people who could talk someday."

"But it does not explain why he kept all this evidence for all these years. If he was worried about someone accusing him of the hit, why not dump the stuff in the river?"

"We've been down this road before. We just go in circles trying to find a rational explanation for why he kept the gun and clothes. Maybe he got a thrill out of having the gun nearby. Trophies, like that horrid set of dog tags and shell casings."

"It's all odd, very odd. If the shell casings were mementos, there isn't one with a nineteen-sixty-three date on it."

They relapse into a long silence again.

"Maybe that's the key—there is no shell casing with November nineteen-sixty-three on it. What if he didn't shoot Kennedy?" Gabby suddenly shouts as she jumps up and begins pacing, throwing out questions like she's cross examining a hostile witness. "First, what if he was contracted to make the hit, so second he goes to Dallas, finds a spot and is lying there waiting for the motorcade when, third, BANG! Oswald shoots.

171

But Galway didn't actually make the hit. Oswald got between him and the job. Now what does he do?

"Four, as his employer—Mafia CIA, whatever—do you want to hear from him again? Does he fear what we suspect— that the employer would want him bumped off, especially if he tried to contact the employer after the event? As the employer you contracted to have the President assassinated and that happened, so why would you contact the guy you hired?

"So Galway's got a target on his back whether he killed Kennedy or not. He can't go to the police and say, 'Hey, I was supposed to kill the President, but Oswald did it first, so protect me from these bad guys who hired me.' And that might explain why he kept his rifle. A ballistic test could rule it out as the weapon used if the police ever tried to pin the killing on him."

"At this point," Glenn counters, "it's still hard not to credit him with involvement."

"Perhaps the final question with which we have to deal is whether there is anyone else out there who believes that Galway was involved. If so, then are we going to be caught in the middle of something not of our making?"

Again they drop into silent thought. Perhaps half an hour elapses before they decide to go into Babcook Manor's air-conditioned comfort. Gabby hoists herself up on the center island in the kitchen while Glenn paces back and forth in front of her.

Glenn finally suggests, "So, back to the transportation issue. If Galway did it, then he had to have driven from Chicago to Dallas."

Suddenly Gabby jumps down and trots out to her car to retrieve her 2007 American Road Atlas, her quick action surprising Glenn. Once back in the kitchen she scrounges a highlighter from a drawer. Opening up to the map of Illinois, she lays the atlas on the granite top of the center island of the gourmet kitchen Glenn covets. She begins to look for routes going south toward Texas.

"Remember," Glenn cautions as he looks over her shoulder, "the Interstates were just being built in sixty-three."

Not seeing anything on the Illinois map that catches her attention, Gabby flips the atlas to Texas, looking for roads that run north from Dallas and that are not Interstates. Then she sees it, traces it north with her finger until she comes to a junction which causes her to moan, "Oh, my God. This can't be."

"What?" a curious Glenn asks as he peers more closely over her shoulder.

"What was the number of that highway that ran from Chicago to California that became famous?"

"Route 66. Ran from Chicago to LA. I think in Illinois today its Interstate 55."

"That's it. 66S 69S 75S!" Gabby exclaims. She uncaps the highlight marker, traces it down the road from Chicago as she recites, "US 66 South to St. Louis. Hmmm? US 66 in Missouri must be Interstate 44 today." Flipping to the map of Missouri she traces from St. Louis to just outside Joplin. "Yeah, US 69 South through Oklahoma." She turns to the Oklahoma map and continues to track. "Yep. At Caddo US 69 becomes US 75 South." Again the atlas pages turn, this time to Texas. The bright orange line tracks down the map until it comes to … Dallas. Gabby looks up at Glenn, whose eyes are still focused on the map. Softly, as if not to be heard, he slowly whispers, "Geeze Louis Gertrude! That's what it means?"

Chapter 51

Before Gabby can answer, as if on cue from the deity in charge of anxiety and tension, the lights go out, literally. Total blackness envelops the Manor. Gabby turns to head toward the switches on the wall by the back door but bumps her knee on the edge of the island.

"Shit and shoved in!" she exclaims.

"You OK?"

"Yeah. Just annoyed at my own carelessness." The flipping of the switches makes no difference in the darkness. Glenn in the meantime moves with care to a window.

"Just what we need on a hot, muggy July night—a general power failure," Gabby moans.

"It's not a general failure. I can see lights in the houses to the west of us. Check the other windows."

Feeling her way, the ache in her knee a constant reminder to go slowly, Gabby makes her way down the hall. "Lights are on in the houses to the east, too. This is very odd, very odd."

"Gabby, there's someone walking up the driveway," Glenn says quietly as he moves into the living room. "You expecting company?"

As quickly as she can without running into a wall, Gabby also makes her way into the living room where Glenn is now standing before the large picture window. Instinctively, both step back from the window and the potential of being seen by the flashlight-wielding person walking quickly toward the house.

"Who the heck do you supposed that is?"

"Our friend in the car across the road? And stupid me, my .45 is in the safe in the apartment," Gabby replies.

"Let's not take any chances. Down to the basement."

They have just reached the bottom of the basement stairs when they hear glass breaking. It sounds like it came from the back kitchen door. *That window's going to need replacing again!* Gabby thinks to herself. There is a crunch of

174

glass on the ceramic tile floor as the intruder moves into the house.

Silently, Glenn moves Gabby toward PWJ's hidden cell. Creeping along very slowly, with outstretched hands to guard against bumping into something that would make noise, they inch along the stairwell wall. Their eyes are becoming accustomed to the dark, but it is still almost impossible to see even the inside of their eyelids.

Once inside the spandrel, Gabby pulls out her cell phone and keys in a text message to the alarm company: "Intruder in house send police ASAP Gordon 3493." As the text is sent, Gabby's phone chimes acknowledgement, the sound echoing off the walls of their lair. Glenn closes the door to their hiding place just as footsteps arrive at the top of the basement stairs.

Gabby silences her phone and holds its face against her chest so that their eyes can re-adjust to the darkness. The sounds of hard leather soles on wood reverberate off the sides of their hiding place as the intruder cautiously descends the stairs. Though they crouch in complete darkness, both instinctively look up toward the source of the overhead sounds.

The intruder reaches the bottom of the stairs and begins to walk across the room, hard leather on concrete, as the stabbing beam of the flashlight makes a pencil-thin line of yellow under the door of their hideaway. It is then that Gabby hears it—the jangling of coins, the unmistakable sound of Scurry! She is leaning forward to open the door to confront him when more footsteps sound from above. The sound of the jangling coins stops and is followed by the click-click of a round being chambered in a gun.

Gabby fears that Scurry has figured out where they are as the sounds of his footsteps near the staircase. Just as the sounds stop, someone at the top of the stairs yells down, "You asshole! Oh, my. You call that a gun? Ha-ha! If you shoot me with that and if I find out about it, I'm gonna stick my foot up your ass!"

Three blasts come in such close proximity that the wood of PWJ's cell hardly masks the deafening reverberations.

A silence follows until the rolling thunder of a body tumbling down the steps fills the gap.

"Did ya find out about that, asshole?" Scurry spits at the crumpled body now at the bottom of the stairs.

Still frozen in place, dust filtering down on them from the impacts of the falling body, Gabby and Glenn wait as the silence stretches into long minutes. Her intent focus on detecting sounds causes Gabby to only slowly become aware of the wetness spreading under her left hand. In her mind a fierce debate ensues over the wisdom of lighting up her cell.

Taking a deep breath while telling herself that it is a deliberate move, not done in panic, she pushes a button and her cell lights up the spandrel. As she recoils from the blood she now sees on her left hand, her legs move, causing the manacles anchored to the wall to also move. *The intruder had to have heard that! So much for rationalizing; turning on the light did attract attention.*

While the cell is still lit, she looks at Glenn, his eyes focusing on her bloody hand. In the dying light as the cell starts to go dark she glances up at the facing wall and sees the letters ICRR stenciled on the backside of the door's paneling. Suddenly oblivious to the blood and the nearing footsteps outside the spandrel, Gabby's mind races as she pieces together an answer to the one remaining riddle from Galway.

Gabby leans over and whispers in Glenn's ear, "Knife." In the darkness she cannot see the surprised look on his face as he reaches down to the sheath on his belt and retrieves it. *Surely, she's not going to try to confront someone with a gun using only a knife?* Glenn thinks. As quietly as he can manage, Glenn opens his knife and places in carefully in Gabby's hands. The light of the cell phone is now completely out.

Though he cannot see what she's doing, Glenn feels Gabby lean toward the door of the spandrel. He is about to reach out to stop her when he hears the sounds of the knife scraping on the wood. The sounds of the footfalls on the steps, however, cover Gabby's effort so that the intruder does not hear her retrieve something from between the paneling and the stair's stringer.

As she sits back against the cement wall, her legs move PWJ's manacles again. They both issue a slight gasp and then hold their breaths awaiting Scurry's move on the spandrel.

"Boss, you 'k?" comes from somewhere in the house, the voice covering the accidental clanking of chains. In the tension of their enclosed space, Scurry's footsteps as he ascends the stairs ring in their ears as if they were inside a kettle drum. Again the distance voice, "Boss, dere is cop cars all over da place. We gotta get. Boss?"

Scurry reaches the top of the stairs and fires three shots into the darkness. As he ducks back from what he thinks will be return fire, his smooth leather soles, now covered with the blood of his victim, slide off a step, throwing him backward. Again the chaotic clamber of a body rumbling down wooden stairs seems to rattle the very walls of the spandrel. Then silence.

"Boss, you down dere? Boss?" Someone is at the top of the stairs.

"Holy shit. Dat prick shot Jimmy."

"Yeah, whose shot da lawyer?"

"Ju shoot?"

"No. Ju?"

"No."

"Whats we gonna do? Cops all over da place out dere."

"Weez got one cherce. Gives up to the cops or shoot it out."

"Dat's two cherces."

"Dere's two cherces. Give up or shoot it out till weez outta ammo, den gets kilt or gives up."

"Look, Gianni. We never fired our guns. Dem two bodies down dere's done kilt demselves. We may get some time for breakin' in, but deres no way weez gonna take a rap for killin' any one."

"Agrees." This is followed by the sounds of two guns sliding across the kitchen floor.

"Don't shoot! Weez givin' up."

The sound of rushing footsteps is followed by the police telling the two men to lie face down with their hands behind their backs. When a pair of policemen come down the steps they call out, "Miss Gordon, it's the police."

Gabby shouts back, "We're in here! We're coming out!" Glenn trips the hidden latch and the door swings open to unmask two beams of light stabbing at their eyes.

"Come on out, Miss Gordon," says one of the officers. "The alarm company said you were somewhere in the house. Come on upstairs. Watch your step around these two."

Gabby can see that a man she assumes is Jimmy the Flea is crumpled at the bottom of the stairs. The pool of blood expanding out from his body shows Scurry's footprints. On top of Jimmy's body is Scurry, his head twisted against the wall, neck obviously broken. Every other step on the way up bares a bloody footprint left by Scurry. At the top of the stairs there is more blood, both on the wall and on the top two steps.

Chapter 52

Gabby and Glenn sit on the patio for over an hour while the police move in and around the house. The adrenalin rush that fortified them with steel nerves to cope during their time under the stairs and the subsequent deaths of two people in such close proximity to their hiding place begins to wear off the longer they sit. Gabby tries to focus her mind on what she can observe of the police and their procedures, while Glenn focuses into himself trying to use meditative practices he once learned while taking a course in Eastern philosophy.

Some sort of mobile command post arrives and a portable generator is started to power flood lights that are placed inside the house. No one speaks to Gabby and Glenn as ambulances and the coroner arrive. State police, sheriff's deputies and Freeport City Police mingle around the outside of the house, all talking in whispers.

The two men who surrendered are seated in the back of separate sheriff's cars while they are being questioned by detective Sumner and a man who turns out to be Chief Deputy Sheriff Joe Morocco.

At length the two investigators come over and sit down opposite Gabby and Glenn.

"We think we have a handle on what happened, but we need to hear your version of events."

Gabby tells of the power failure and seeing a man approaching, and of how they hid in the basement. She tells what they heard of the confrontation between the two men, the shooting and then the falls.

Glenn's version of the events matches Gabby's.

"The comment about finding out about being shot is curious. The man we ID'ed as Scurry was using a Beretta Bobcat pistol, which fires .22 caliber longs. Compared to the 9mm Glock the man we ID'ed as Jimmy 'the Flea' Donati had on him, the Beretta may have appeared to be a toy," Chief Deputy Morocco notes wryly.

"Scurry must not have been experienced with a pistol. One slug hit Jimmy in the right arm just below the elbow. Another nicked his neck and the carotid artery. That's why he bled so much before falling. The final shot impacted in the door frame above his head," Detective Sumner adds. "Classic pattern of the gun's aim moving up from the recoil of each successive shot."

"Frick and Frack over there," Morocco throws a thumb over his shoulder toward the cars with the other two men in it, "have given preliminary statements which corroborate what you've told us."

"Scurry owed Jimmy three hundred thousand dollars from some gambling debts," Gabby adds. "One of Jimmy's heavies, a guy named Schicchi, showed up here a couple days ago looking for Scurry and he mentioned the debt."

"That also jibes with what Frick and Frack said. Any idea why Scurry broke in here?"

"He was trying to get access to the bank account of John Galway. Since I was Galway's attorney, he must have figured that I could be forced to give him the code."

Detective Sumner looks at Deputy Morocco, "Galway was shot with a .22. You suppose Scurry shot Galway?"

"His Beretta has threading on the barrel for a sound suppressor. Bet we find one in his car. That thing would have been bigger and heavier than the Beretta. Had to be tough to aim with any accuracy, especially for a guy who has trouble aiming anyway."

"Jimmy's Glock hadn't been fired. Not too smart for a debt collector to go into a dark house with your gun in the small of your back if you think the other guy's packin'."

"None of these guys seem like they'd be candidates for Mensa," Glenn opines.

"Be nice to wrap this up in a neat package. Three dead and no murder trial to generate months of paperwork. What about Frick and Frack?"

"We got 'em on breaking and entering. That'll get 'em each a few years."

"It'll also make the State's Attorney happy as it would put a couple notches on his belt from of all this. The murderer who trips and falls to his death doesn't rack up publicity for somebody who needs to get re-elected periodically."

The local electric company—Com Ed—reconnects the power just as the police finish questioning Gabby and Glenn. Soon everyone is gone but a lone deputy posted at the end of the driveway to keep out the curious. Gabby figures with the Fourth of July holiday the next day it will be Monday before anyone from the State Crime lab comes to process the scene. Not having experience in criminal matters, she is surprised when the crime scene people arrive within the hour.

Chapter 53

With the State Crime Lab personnel on the scene, Gabby and Glenn go up to her apartment, the air-conditioned interior just beginning to reach a tolerable point now that the power has been restored. Gabby makes two cups of coffee on her Keurig and they sit down at the kitchen table.

"What was all that with my knife? I thought you were going to confront Scurry with it."

"Oh," exclaims Gabby. "I forgot with the shooting and Scurry's fall. When I lit up my cell to find out what was on my hand, I saw the letters 'ICRR' branded into the back side of the paneling. Then I remembered what Barnes told me about Babcook's personal rail car and him using the paneling down in the basement."

"But how did you know to look there?" Glenn asks.

"I forgot to tell you that Galway enclosed a note for me in his Will. He said if we wanted to find the final answers we had to make the connections between 'Freeport, TR, TNT, RR, and PWJ.' When I saw the brand on the paneling it hit me. Freeport, Teddy Roosevelt, the bomb on the Chicago and Alton line and the place where Babcook, Junior was imprisoned. That had to be the location. I also recalled that the dust pattern on the floor in there was too neat and had a flow from left to right?"

Gabby reaches back under her shirt to pull out an envelope from the small of her back. She lays it on the table between them. Both stare at it for a long time. There is no writing on the outside. Glenn turns it over and sees that it is sealed. He reaches for the knife he usually carries on his belt, but it is gone. He looks at Gabby quizzically.

"Oh, I'm sorry, I left it lying on the floor of PWJ's cell."

"That means that the Crime Lab people will grab it in case its evidence. I'll never see it again."

"I promise I'll buy you a new one."

182

Leaning back on his chair so that he can reach the drawer where Gabby keeps utensils, he retrieves another knife. Carefully he slits the envelop open and removes the contents: two passports and a folded piece of paper.

Picking up the passports, he examines them saying, "one is in the name of John Galway and the other is in the name of a Sean O'Fallon.' Did you catch the minor name change? Well, both expired in sixty-eight. Both have entrance visa stamps for Italy dated January twenty-fourth, nineteen sixty-two. Only the Sean O'Fallon passport has an exit stamp from Italy, and that is dated January twenty-six, of the same year."

Gabby, while listening to Glenn, unfolds the letter that was with the passports.

"Well, wait till you hear this," she begins:

To the finder of this letter: I presume that I'm dead if this has been found, at least I hope so. All my life I have been a sniper—a hunter of men. I worked mostly for the Mafia. In '62 I was sent to Italy to kill Charles Luciano. The hit was to end the power struggle over control of the Cosa Nostra in the US. Luciano, who had been deported from the US to Italy, seldom was ever in a public place, but he was supposed to meet an American film producer in the airport in Naples and I was to hit him as he left. For this I was paid $3 million in advance. As it turned out, Luciano died of a heart attack while in the airport. The Cosa Nostra had provided me with an escort while in Italy, and I figured he was supposed to knock me off after I made the hit. When Luciano croaked, I had to kill my guide and jump the next plane out. Fearing for my life and that of my wife, I have spent all the years since hiding in this basement. [Signed] Sean Fallon.

"Well, I guess we were way off-base," sighs Glenn. "The whole Kennedy thing was some sort of a ruse. Too bad. In my head I was already writing a book about it."

"Charles Luciano? What was that name that Kelstead called Galway that got the old man so angry? 'Lucky,' that's it.

183

So that's why Kelstead upset him with the off-hand comment about 'Lucky Luciano.' He did have something to fear, even if it was just someone wanting their money back," Gabby reasons aloud.

"Do you suppose those numbers and letters on that piece of newsprint were intentionally misleading?"

"Probably. Who knows? Galway must have slowly gone nuts living down in the basement, so he may have concocted all sorts of ruses and red herrings to throw off anyone who might come snooping around. Or maybe it was his way of amusing himself—creating clues and answers that pointed to some hit he would like to have made. Who knows?"

"So, based on his father-in-law's Will, Mary Alice got four million as her inheritance and then Galway got three million for a hit that never happened. That would explain the two different Swiss bank accounts. One had to be kept hidden for fear that someone in the Cosa Nostra might find him through his wife. Do you suppose that is the one with all the money still in it?"

"Could be. The Cosa Nostra would have known about the account they put the hit money in, but he would have wanted to provide for his wife in the event he died first,"

"I'll bet he immediately moved the money from the account that the Cosa Nostra knew about, but he might have been afraid that they might get the Swiss bankers to reveal that new account."

"So he left information in the safety deposit box about the UBS account in case his wife needed it. But it still doesn't explain why he kept all the stuff he hid around here."

"We may never know the answer to that question, and we may yet uncover more," a weary Gabby concludes.

FINIAL

B efore they leave, one of the Crime Lab technicians talks to Gabby and gives her a piece of paper with the names and contact numbers of companies who specialize in cleaning crime scenes where blood is involved. Once the Crime Lab technicians leave, it is a very tired Gabby and Glenn who trudge over to the couch in her apartment. Glenn wraps his arms around her as they sit. Neither one speaks for over an hour as they try to process all that has happened. Finally, still holding each other, they lay down side by side Gabby nestling into Glenn's embrace.

When Glenn speaks, he whispers, "You can't sell the house now, we've got too much history with it to let it go."

"But I can't afford the payments, let alone the insurance, taxes and putting some kind of furniture in it."

"Excuse me, but aren't you the lady who just inherited over twelve million dollars from some crackpot who put you through hell? And didn't his Will state that the money was to be used to take care of Babcook Manor?"

"I thought she got four million from the Flaherty's estate."

"How much interest do you suppose four million dollars would accumulate in over fifty years in a Swiss bank account?"

"I guess you're right about that. So, money is not the question anymore. What really worries me is that the house has been a prison for everyone who ever lived there, and it's awfully big for just the—ahhh—two of us."

"Oh, the two of us? Well, that's forward thinking, to say the least. Yes I guess for just the two of us, but we could fill some of those rooms with little architects and attorneys."

There is a long pause, which begins to make Glenn nervous the longer it lasts, so he adds, "I'm just sayin' because you said…."

Gabby, a broad smile on her face, turns to look at Glenn, "Is that a proposal, soon-to-be ex-Cardinal fan?"

"Sounds like one to me."

"Hmmmm, so you think a geeky architect and a hammer-wielding attorney can make a go of it? Well, then I see no reason to object." Gabby kisses him before rolling back to cuddle deeper in his arms.

"Besides," Glenn continues, "we'll need a place to live while we tackle our next project."

"What next project?"

"Well, I have my eye on this building in downtown Freeport that would make a good office on the first floor and a couple of incoming-producing apartments on the second and third floors. But it does need some major work."

"I'll take that under advisement."

As he kisses her ear he whispers, "Counselor, I rest my case."

About an hour later Gabby is still awake but she can tell from the rhythm of Glenn's breathing that he has fallen asleep. Carefully, so as not to wake him, she untwines from his arms and tiptoes to the window looking down on Babcook Manor. As she stands there, gazing at the house in the aubergine glow of the early dawn, she thinks: *It was a prison for PWJ, then for Ethel and then Galway. We will have to make sure it is never again someone's prison.*

cknowledgements

The following individuals provided valuable suggestion and comments on this work while in manuscript form:

My fellow Caxton Book Club members: Becky Connors, Mary Hartman, Jennifer Kanosky, Teresa Julius, and Shawn Shianna.

Others who reviewed all or parts of the manuscript included: Geoff Rodkey, Bonnie Curran, Nicole M. Bauer-Greene, and Keith & Diane Martin.

For valuable advice thanks to Terri Reid.

Emily Herren deserves singular recognition for her efforts to end my love affair with the comma.

A special thanks to my daughter Remy Finch Garard for her guidance and support.

Finally, to my wife Cathy, my grateful appreciation for being both my first reader and my greatest source of encouragement and support.

But in the end, any mistakes are my own.

EFF
Freeport, Illinois
30 April 2015

Previously Published by Edward F. Finch

Beneath the Waves: The Life and Navy of CAPT. Edward L. Beach, Jr. Naval Institute Press, 2010. [www.nip.org]

NB: Winchilsea Press neither solicits nor accepts manuscripts or submissions.

Coming Soon

Tumbling Blocks
The second Gabby Gordon mystery

Made in the USA
Middletown, DE
29 May 2015